FATHER TO THE MAN

a novel by

Barbara J. Olexer

Joyous Publishing
Milwaukie, Oregon

The boy is father to the man. – Old Adage

Copyright © 2009
by Barbara J. Olexer

Cover photo of Ashland, Oregon
by Fred Stockwell
www.stockwellphotos.com

ISBN 978-0-9800514-1-4

Large Print (16 point)
Joyous Publishing
www.joyouspub.com

Printed in the U.S.A.

Books by Barbara J. Olexer

Novels

They Lived Ever After
Death Takes a Flyer
Murder by Accident
If You Can't Trust Your Uncle Sam
Fossil Rocks
Father to the Man
Criminal Justice

Nonfiction

Presidential Education: Prelude to Power
The Enslavement of the American Indian
in Colonial Times
Murder of a Soul: The Story of
Captain Jack (film biography)
What Astrology Means to You: A Handbook of
Astrological Terms, Glyphs, and Applications

FOREWORD

Ashland is a real town and it is really situated in southern Oregon. Most of the geography of Ashland and its environs is correctly given in these pages. I have taken creative license, however, with the high school and its sports program. I have no idea how the school is organized, whether it is a consolidated school or remains a city school.

I lived in Ashland for a couple of years in the early fifties; I was a child. and loved it greatly. Lithia Park, the Plaza, the dignified old library, the college, George A. Briscoe Elementary School, Walker Elementary School, Twin Plunges, the Shakespeare Festival – all these are still fresh in my memory bank.

Barbara J. Olexer
Milwaukie, Oregon

CHAPTER 1

Keith and Kurt Kovacek came out of the Jackson County Courthouse into the gray drizzly light of an early autumn day. Keith was fuming but Kurt was philosophical. Of course, the judge had fined Keith, which made it pretty easy for Kurt to be philosophical about it. As they made their way through the parking lot, Kurt fished his keys out. Climbing in behind the wheel of their jointly owned and lovingly restored 1957 Chevy, Kurt started her up and grinned at his glowering twin.

"You got to learn to roll with the punches, man," he advised. "Justice system's set up to protect society from desperadoes like you. You infringed, you got popped, you learn your lesson."

"Pop's gonna go ballistic," Keith grumbled. "And as for justice, you tell me where there's any justice in a cop hiding out and then nailing a guy for speeding. Practically enticement and entrapment, if you ask me. Besides which, I wasn't even speeding that night."

Kurt pulled out and merged into the traffic. "Well, bro, you got to admit you violated the basic rule."

Keith snarled. "Basic rule! Oh, yeah, makes a lot of sense. They can't get you any other way, they throw in the basic rule. That way they can get you for anything, guilty or not."

Kurt laughed, then said, "I have to agree with you. The basic rule is a damn vague piece of law. And hiding out that way is the next thing to entrapment and if my memory serves me, the U.S. Supreme Court is all against entrapment."

"Damn right. So's anyone except the damn cops."

"You know, we ought to give ol' Simple Simon a little lesson in civic responsibility."

Keith cheered up a bit. "That's a thought. You got anything specific in mind?"

"Not specific, no. But I've got a sort of glimmering of an idea."

The boys had been involved in a feud with Officer Simonson since the previous spring. They felt that he interfered with their pursuit of happiness with arrogant glee and undue enthusiasm. There was a dilapidated old barn at the edge of an alfalfa field that fronted on a stretch of highway that the boys often traveled. The highway patrolman, Bob Simonson, whose duty it was to foil evil-doers along that piece of the public thoroughfare, often parked inside the open doors of the barn and waited for his prey -- speeders, unsafe passers, tailgaters. All violators of the traffic code could expect short shrift from the zealous lawman. The twins' buddy, Jazzy Janowski, had named the officer Simple Simon one night when he had stopped the boys for speeding.

Keith had happened to be driving and the speedometer registered 50 mph when he heard the siren behind him and looked up to see flashing red and blue lights in his rearview mirror. The posted speed limit was 55 but it was raining heavily, which brought him into violation of the basic rule. Oregon's basic rule states that regardless of the posted speed limit, a driver may be found guilty of speeding if road and/or weather conditions warrant a lesser speed. Keith's date, Carla Springer, was boning up to try for her driver's license and had left a motor vehicles department driver's manual on the back seat. Kurt and Keith had gotten out of the car and taken turns reading irrelevant bits of the manual to Officer Simonson, liberally interjecting their own comments and criticisms.

Then, too, their twinship being of the identical type, they had pulled their razzle-dazzle routine of who's who, giving the good Simonson the temporary impression that there were about six of the Kovacek twins, all of whom claimed to be models of deportment and discretion. In the end, Simonson had got tired of standing out in the rain listening to nonsense and had disgustedly issued a citation to Keith, pretty much at random as he had completely lost track of which twin had been driving. As they drove away, Jazzy had thoughtfully remarked that ol' Simonson was sure a simple bastard, and the name had stuck.

Keith and Kurt lived in Ashland, Oregon, where their parents had a thriving office products store just off the Plaza. The Janowskis owned a ranch at the foot of Mt. Mazama out of Fort Klamath. Except for the long-forgotten Pole who had contributed the family surname, all the Janowskis were members of the Klamath Indian Tribe. In order to get Jazzy, who had been named Melvin Leroy, away from the prejudice of the local whites, his parents had decided to send him to board with the Kovaceks and attend the Ashland school. The two families had become friends through the distaff side. Dextra Kovacek and Marie Janowski had been roommates at Southern Oregon College when "of Education" had been part of its name. They had remained close, getting together frequently so that the three boys had grown up together.

All three were good-looking, dark haired and brown eyed. The twins were tall, right at the six-foot mark, and rangy. Jazzy was square-built and looked deceptively like an immovable object, which gave him an edge on the football field because his opponents were always surprised that he could run like an antelope. Jazzy lived with the Kovaceks through the week and Keith and Kurt often went home with him on weekends.

The twins stopped at the mall on their way home from the court house to pick up a suit for their mother. She'd left it at Shea's for alterations and had asked them to retrieve it for her. Keith peeled off at Sonny's Sports to price ski boots, both boys having outgrown the ones from the previous winter. Kurt went into the women's wear shop and was looking around for a saleslady when he spotted Merrilee Corbin. He and Merrilee had gone steady their sophomore and junior years but Kurt had broken it off during the summer. Merrilee had been terribly hurt but had tried gallantly to hide her pain and had succeeded so well that not even Kurt, who was still deeply in love with her, was aware that her world still revolved around him.

He had steeled himself to see and meet her with equanimity at school but, unexpectedly catching sight of her just then, Kurt stopped abruptly and merely stood and looked. She was wearing a formal, a swirling gown of ice blue chiffon and lace. Even the sulky expression on her face could not spoil the lovely picture she made. The icy blue set off her light brown, shoulder-length hair and complemented the blue of her eyes. Had Kurt thought for a moment, he would have realized that she was shopping for a gown to wear to the homecoming game, having been acclaimed one of the princesses. But he didn't think, he only saw his darling looking perfectly delectable and as far out of his reach as if they'd been on different continents. That the situation was of his own making had no effect on the depth of his yearning.

"It's not exactly what I had in mind, Mom," Merrilee said in a way that acknowledged her inability to affect her mother's intention that she wear that gown and no other.

Kurt frowned as Mrs. Corbin stood up and went to her daughter.

"No doubt," she said acidly. "I'm sure what you had in mind was one of those backless, mini-skirted, nearly topless things. But as long as you live in my house, you'll wear decent clothes."

As Merrilee turned toward her mother, she saw Kurt standing a couple of racks away. She stood looking at him with longing in her eyes, almost a perfect reflection of his look at her.

Mrs. Corbin turned to see what had caught her daughter's attention and her face, already sour, became positively bitter as she recognized Kurt.

"Go and take it off," Mrs. Corbin ordered, spinning Merrilee around and giving her a little push toward the dressing room.

Merrilee went without protest, followed by the saleslady. Mrs. Corbin stood and glared at Kurt as he went on his way.

Ashland's school district had been amalgamated and, like high schools all over America, Pioneer Consolidated High School had a football team. Also like all high school football teams, the Pumas fielded players of varying abilities, some good, some okay, some pretty dismal, and a very few pretty darn good. The stars of this team were Kurt and Keith Kovacek and their buddy, Jazzy Janowski. All three were seniors. The homecoming game was the final of the season and would be the boys' last high school football game. They were determined to win it. They would be playing their arch-rivals and the boys considered it imperative for the sake of their honor, the honor of the team, and the honor of the school that the three of them lead the team to victory.

Coach Blaine was new to Pioneer High that year and had begun badly with the team. He was the kind of overweight, out-of-shape coach who bullied his team into obedience rather than helping them to develop their own talents and styles. Ashland had been fortunate in the previous coach, a solid all-around man named Cramer, who had retired after nearly thirty years of coaching Puma teams to a number of state championships, not only in football but in the other sports as well. Kurt was quarterback, Jazzy was offensive captain and Keith was an offensive running back when Blaine started the football season with them and they had three very good seasons behind them. Coach Blaine was not fond of any of them and was, in fact, outright hostile to the two Kovaceks. But his own well-being depended to a large extent on the team's win-loss record and if he was ever going to get out of small-time coaching and into a school that could afford to pay bigger bucks (and where he wouldn't have to teach health and freshman math), he needed a winning season. So he had put his own antipathies aside in appointing leadership roles.

The night before the game, the three boys were in the twins' room, ostensibly doing their homework, in reality planning their strategy for the game. They were convinced that they knew better than Blaine and they planned to do their own thing in this last game. It would almost certainly cost them their places on the basketball and baseball teams, not to mention wrestling for Kurt and track for Jazzy, but football was the main thing and they meant to show Blaine what a fool he'd been all this time by insisting on his own plays when they were inferior to those of the triumvirate.

"If Donnelly and Ivorson don't lose their heads," Kurt said, "I don't see how we can go wrong. All they have to do is block so we can run the ball. The Spartans don't have much of an offensive team but they're pretty damn good on defense."

Jazzy and Keith nodded.

"Well, Kurt, take care of your throwing arm." Jazzy said seriously. "No amount of blocking is going to do any good if you can't throw the ball."

"My arm's all right," Kurt growled.

"Sure, it's just fine," Keith agreed ironically. "That's why you threw the ball the whole entire distance of twenty yards at practice today. Twice."

"Oh, shut up. It's just a little sore. I was saving it for tomorrow." Kurt glared at his brother and then at Jazzy.

"Uh-huh. Well, keep saving it."

Jazzy reached out for a slab of Dextra's chocolate brownie, rich with chopped walnuts.

"Hey," Keith demanded of his brother, "pass me the brownies."

Kurt was sitting on the carpet, leaning against his bed, where Jazzy was sprawled, eating brownies and swigging milk. Keith was on his own bed, sitting cross-legged with an enormous German beer stein full of ice and cola. Jeb, Kurt's Golden Labrador Retriever, and Sam, Keith's Irish Setter, were lying alertly on the floor between the beds, watching hopefully for any sign that the boys intended to share their snack.

Kurt broke the remaining brownie in half and passed the pan to Keith.

"You're going pretty hot and heavy with Jackie," Keith admonished his brother. "You better cool it or you'll find yourself at the end of her old man's shotgun."

Kurt's temper flared. "At least I'm not going to end up married to Carla Springer. You're the one better cool it."

"Oh, man," Keith said, "I'm careful. I'm real careful."

"I don't know what you see in that woman," Jazzy said, shaking his head sadly. "She isn't even good looking."

"She puts out," Kurt said.

"That's all she's got going for her," Jazzy said.

"We can't all have someone like Lora devoted to us," Keith said. "I swear I don't see what a gorgeous woman like her sees in an old broken-down cowpoke like you."

Jazzy threw a pillow at Keith. "She loves me because I'm sensitive."

Both twins howled derisively.

"Oh, yeah," Kurt agreed, "you're sensitive. It must be all that sensitivity that made you nearly break your hand on Massy's jaw that time."

Jazzy grinned sheepishly. "In a kind of way, it was. If he hadn't been giving Rosalie a hard time, I wouldn't have punched his lights out. Anyway," he added pugnaciously, "at least I know there's more to women than pussy."

"I've heard you say so," Keith agreed. "But I can't say I've seen too much indication of it, myself."

"You'll fall in love one of these fine days," Kurt said. "And when you do, you'll fall hard."

Rudy Kovacek paused in the open doorway. He, like his sons, was a handsome man. His hair was mostly white but he still walked tall and there was plenty of authority in his voice, soft-spoken as he was. "You boys finished with your homework?"

The three boys looked at him with expressions of seraphic virtue.

"Time for bed, is it, Pop?" Keith asked.

Dextra slipped into the room and reached for the empty brownie pan but Jazzy snatched it up.

"I'll take it down and put it to soak, Dextra," he said.

He piled the milk glasses into the pan and picked up the empty milk jug.

"Thank you, Jazzy," Dextra said, smiling at him. The twins' mother was small and beginning to plump up after forty-odd years of slenderness. She had never been a beautiful woman but her face was pleasant and her smile was delightful.

Jazzy went downstairs amid a flurry of goodnights as Dextra and Rudy went down the hall to their room. The dogs followed Jazzy down, ever hopeful of human generosity in the matter of snacks.

It was evident during the first quarter of the homecoming game that Kurt had spoken truly when he said his arm was all right. Keith was usually Kurt's receiver of choice, not entirely from brotherly prejudice; the statistics bore him out that Keith caught a bigger percentage of passes than any of the others. Keith just seemed to know in advance where to be when Kurt let fly with the ball. Jazzy was wide receiver and the three had played together so much that he was nearly as adept as Keith at being in position when Kurt threw the ball. They only half-way listened to the coach's harangue as they suited up and disregarded all of it as they hit the field. The drizzle had lasted most of the week and the field was saturated, with water standing in the low spots.

The Pumas won the toss and Kurt elected to receive. Keith caught the ball and ran it for a respectable gain before the other side tackled him and brought him down. A few more plays brought them within striking distance of their goalposts and Kurt called the team into a huddle. Coach Blaine was making urgent signals from the sidelines but Kurt ignored him and gave the team the play of his own choice. Coach turned bright red with fury when he saw the team go into formation.

Kurt received the ball from the center's snap, faded back and looked for his receiver. Keith had been brought down by a man who'd been tackling him at every opportunity, no matter what the play. Jazzy was open, although in a perilous spot, so Kurt threw the ball to him. Jazzy began his turn even before the ball got to him, snatched it out of the air and was out of reach when the nearest man jumped for him. He slipped a little on the wet grass but so did the two guys who were chasing him, one of whom went down; the other made a dive and brought Jazzy down just one step inside the end zone.

The Spartans held them to the one touchdown in the first quarter but Keith and Joe Ivorson each made a touchdown in the second quarter.

Coach Blaine looked far more like the opposing coach, halfway through the game with a score of 21 to zip, than like the winning coach. Egos run amuck in American sports, just as much (or even more) at the high school level as at the professional level. Fortunately, the homecoming half-time ceremonies kept coach and rebels apart for most of the interval or something regrettable might have been said or done. As it was, Keith took his place as escort for one of the Homecoming Princesses while Jazzy, as escort for Rita Jameson, the Homecoming Queen, presented her with an armful of pink roses. Kurt stood with the rest of the team and had eyes only for Merrilee.

The cold drizzle, the wet field, and the half-time ceremonies had combined to take the edge off both teams when the third quarter began. They played some lackluster ball, both sides feeling that they needed snorkels to play and neither side scoring until halfway through the quarter, when the Spartans made a touchdown and followed it with a two-point conversion. They followed that with another touchdown, but missed on the extra point. Kurt happened to glance at Coach Blaine and saw that he was looking distinctly more cheerful, almost smug, in fact. With a shock, Kurt realized that it was because the coach was anticipating their chagrin at losing a game they had committed mutiny in order to play their own way. That brought him to and he gave the team a pep talk when they huddled.

Just as they broke from the huddle, Norbert Halsey trotted onto the field and proudly announced that Coach had sent him in to replace Keith. Kurt laughed and sent him back to the bench. It wasn't that Halsey was such a poor player, although he was not anywhere near as good as Keith, it was that both Kovaceks, as well as the rest of the team, knew it was meant to embarrass Keith and, by extension, Kurt. Halsey was humiliated to the depths of his sophomore being but the incident had the effect of galvanizing the Pioneer team. More than ever determined to show Blaine that he was a detriment to their playing, they hurled themselves against their foes.

Kurt moved laterally behind the line of scrimmage, looking for a receiver. Keith materialized in the exact spot where Kurt needed him to be and Kurt let fly with the ball. It was a little high but Keith leaped for it, caught it, and splashed his way over the goal line as his team-mates neutralized the efforts of the other team. A couple of plays later, knowing that the Spartans would be expecting him to throw either to Keith or Jazzy, Kurt handed off to Tom Loughlin and

Tom ran the ball over the goal line. They kept the Spartans from scoring the rest of the quarter and the Spartans held them back until the final minutes of the game.

Kurt knew if he was ever going to find out whether he or Blaine was right about his ability to make a certain play, it was now or never. In spite of the fact that half the team would have forgotten it, never having actually used it, he called the play. Putting his trust in the natural impulse of his teammates to stop the opposition, when the center snapped the ball Kurt tucked it under his arm, put his head down and charged straight through the line. It went off like clockwork, as if they'd practiced it daily all season long. He threw the ball down in the end zone, splashing up a fountain of water and went into a victory dance. The rest of the team rushed him, coming from the field and the sidelines, and the Pioneer High students jumped down from the stands and splashed in amongst the team, screaming and cheering.

CHAPTER 2

Highly stoked after the game, the team erupted from the locker room onto the parking lot. Keith, Carla, Jazzy, Lora, and Kurt piled into the twins' Chevy, with Kurt at the wheel. Lora Wilder was a lovely girl. Like Jazzy, she was a Klamath Indian. She wore her hair long and unbound, her skin had a rosy glow, and her dark brown eyes sparkled, hinting at the depths of emotion that she kept hidden from all but those dearest to her. Carla Springer just missed being a pretty girl. Her dishwater blond hair was frizzy and her light blue eyes were a shade too close together.

The kids rolled all the windows down and drove up and down the main drag several times with the other kids celebrating their victory, horns honking, shouting, laughing, and yelling. Then Kurt took the highway north, out of town.

Out in the suburbs, down a side street, there was a nice old man who sold them beer and occasionally vodka, which they fondly believed left no tell-tale odor on the breath. It was more convenient than faked I.D. and not nearly so apt to get anyone in trouble. Plus, it gave the old guy a few bucks to supplement his social security check. The next stop was a convenience store for orange juice to mix with the vodka. Kurt and Jazzy went in, leaving the others in the car.

As they came out, laughing at something witty that Jazzy had said, Norbert Halsey stepped out of the shadows and stood in front of Kurt, dangling an open beer bottle in his right hand. Halsey was nearly as tall as Kurt, with a heavier build. It was obvious that in addition to being in a furious temper, he was more than half drunk.

"Shut up, Kovacek. I've had enough of you."

Kurt stood and looked Halsey over. Keith came around to stand behind his brother while Jazzy watched the others to see if Halsey was acting alone or with some of his pals.

"Well, well," said Kurt. "What have we here? Mrs. Halsey's baby boy is still trying to play with the big kids."

Halsey threw the beer bottle down right in front of Kurt, where it smashed, spraying beer and splinters of glass in every direction.

"I said shut up," Halsey shouted.

"Are you going to make me shut up, Halsey?" Kurt asked quietly.

"Damn you! Damn you! Yes! I'm going to

make you shut up."

Halsey was so angry that he forgot any boxing science he'd ever learned, which wasn't much. Not nearly as much as he thought he had. He hit Kurt a glancing blow on the shoulder and Kurt replied with a quick one-two to the body. Halsey staggered back and steadied himself. He pulled a K-bar knife from the sheath under his coat and as it glinted in the light, Merrilee ran from behind a nearby car and screamed. Lora caught her and pulled her to a stop. Merrilee looked at her and grasped her hand, holding it tightly. Keith started forward.

"Keep out of it, Keith," Kurt rasped.

Keith stopped. Kurt whipped his jacket off and wrapped it around his arm. Merrilee drew in her breath for another scream but Lora clamped her hand over her mouth.

"Stop that," Jazzy ordered, glaring at Merrilee. "Do you want to get him killed?"

Merrilee shook her head and Lora took her hand away; Merrilee continued to hold onto Lora. Jazzy stood close to her just in case.

Halsey's father had been a Marine and Halsey had often heard him describe and demonstrate the uses of a K-bar. But Mr. Halsey had never actually instructed his son in the art of knife fighting, although Halsey considered himself trained. He crouched in the approved manner, moving in an arc a cautious distance from Kurt.

Halsey lunged forward suddenly and made a swipe with the knife. Kurt jumped back, out of his reach, then sprang forward, using his wrapped arm to fend off the knife as he drove his fist into Halsey's solar plexus. Halsey went down, dropping the knife and clutching at his stomach with both hands. Kurt kicked the knife away and someone picked it up, he didn't see who.

Merrilee broke away from Jazzy and ran to Kurt.

"You're bleeding," she sobbed. "Oh, Kurt, oh, Kurt."

Kurt looked at his arm and saw that his jacket had slipped so that it offered no protection at all.

"How bad is it?" Keith asked. "You want to go to the hospital? Get it sewed up?"

"Hell no," Kurt said. "I don't think it's deep. Come on, let's get out of here."

Halsey was on his knees, retching violently. A couple of his pals were standing behind him, trying to think what to do. The rest of the on-lookers were chattering about the excitement. Merrilee was wearing a plaid skirt and yellow twin-set sweaters. She tore her coat off then the cardigan and wrapped the sweater around Kurt's arm.

"Hey, the blood will ruin it," Kurt exclaimed.

Merrilee held it firmly in place. "It doesn't matter. We'd better go to my house. We can wash the blood off and see if you need to go to the hospital."

The others all stood still and stared at her. She tugged at Kurt impatiently.

"Come on," she cried.

"I don't want to get you in trouble again," Kurt protested.

"My folks aren't home. They've gone to the Kirkpatricks' for dinner and they always play pinochle half the night afterwards. Will you come on?"

Keith and Kurt exchanged glances while Jazzy and Lora shook their heads at this turn of events. Kurt shrugged and started for the car.

Merrilee ran over to a girlfriend.

"Cheryl, I've got to go with Kurt. Tell your mom and dad that I didn't feel well and that I went home, will you?"

Cheryl nodded. "I think you're crazy, Merrilee. Nothing but trouble is ever going to come out of messing with Kurt Kovacek. But I'll cover for you as much as I can."

"Thanks."

Merrilee dashed over to the Kovaceks' car and slid into the back seat beside Kurt. Jazzy and Lora were also in the back seat.

"What was that all about?" Merrilee asked.

"Oh, Halsey got all bent out of shape during the game tonight. He's been upset with me for awhile and tonight evidently pushed him over the edge."

Carla twisted around on the front seat. "Well, can you blame him? You took Lois Beeman away from him a couple of months ago and you never pass up a chance to make him look like a fool."

Kurt cast a quick, guilty glance at Merrilee.

"Shut up, Carla," Keith ordered. "Mind your own business."

Carla cast an angry glance at Keith and started to answer him but Lora forestalled her.

"Keith," she said, speaking softly as she always spoke, "Maybe you should drop Jazzy and me off at his pickup. We still have to get over the mountain tonight."

"Yeah," Jazzy seconded her. "If you don't need us, we'd best get on home."

"I'm okay," Kurt assured them. "It's not deep. Merrilee will work a little of her magic on it and I'll be fine."

After they dropped Jazzy and Lora off at his old and somewhat battered pickup, Keith drove to Merrilee's home. They trooped into the kitchen and Merrilee sat Kurt down at the kitchen table and brought materials for cleaning and bandaging the cut, which was shallow.

"You ought to have some stitches, Kurt," Merrilee insisted, sponging the blood away.

"I'm all right. Just bandage it."

"Keith, look at it. Make him go to the hospital."

Keith worriedly looked at the cut, searched his brother's face, and shrugged. "Hey, if he says he doesn't need stitches, he doesn't need any. Mom and Pop have enough to worry about already."

Keith pulled Carla away from her avid examination of Kurt's wound and sat her down on his lap at one end of the table, so Merrilee's back was to them. As Keith and Carla necked, Merrilee sprayed disinfectant on Kurt's arm, making him jump.

"Ow, that stings like hell," he complained.

"I know, but it's got to be done," Merrilee said.

"I think you enjoyed it," Kurt accused her.

"No. I don't want to hurt you, Kurt."

Kurt watched her face as she bandaged his arm. She put her bloody sweater and the bloody towels she'd used in a plastic trash bag, then gathered up the first aid materials, ignoring Keith and Carla.

Kurt followed her into the bathroom where she put the first aid spray and bandaging gauze and adhesive tape in the medicine chest. He put his good arm around her and kissed the back of her neck.

"Merrilee?" he questioned softly.

She turned and put her arms around his neck. "Oh, Kurt. I've been so miserable."

"I know. I'm sorry. I've been pretty miserable, too."

"I just couldn't understand, you know. Why you suddenly quit calling me and didn't want to talk to me or anything. I still don't understand."

"Merrilee," he murmured her name into her hair, holding her close.

He kissed her, at first softly and gently but with increasing passion. She allowed the kisses but didn't return them. He pulled his head back and looked into her eyes questioningly.

"Why, Kurt?"

"Because I love you so much," he said.

The look of incredulity on her face drove him to explain.

"I was afraid of you, Merrilee. I don't want to get married right out of high school -- or still in high school. You're a good girl, you're the light of my life -- if you got pregnant, I'd have to marry you. And there are things I need to do first."

Instead of looking as if she understood, Merrilee looked more puzzled than ever. Then anger became her principle emotion. Seeing that,

Kurt tried to explain his feelings again, as she stepped away from him, folding her arms across her midriff.

"Don't be mad, try to understand. I love you and I want you but I don't want to hurt you. If you love me, sooner or later we're going to have sex. And in spite of all precautions, you might get pregnant. Abortion would be out of the question so we'd have to get married. What about college, then? You want to be a teacher and I want to be an engineer. So I thought the best thing was to cool it with you. See?"

Merrilee was still angry but she was beginning to understand. "I think you're taking an awful lot for granted, Kurt. I have no intention of having sex with you or anyone else before I'm married. You're right, I do have plans to go to college and become a teacher. After that, I'll think about marriage -- not before."

"I'm sorry," Kurt said desperately. "Merrilee, I'm sorry. I guess I did take too much for granted. Maybe you don't love me. But that's what I thought and that's what I felt. I was only trying to do what's best for you."

Merrilee's expression softened and she dropped her arms to her sides. "Okay, I accept that," she said. "You'd better go, now. If my folks come home early, we'll all be in big trouble. You know how they feel about you."

"Yeah, I know. They hate my guts."

They went out into the hall and Merrilee turned off the bathroom light as she left. The only light came from the kitchen so the hall was dim. At the foot of the stairs Kurt stopped and held his hand out to her. She stepped into the circle of his arm and kissed him. He was lost in the wonder of her when an incautious movement of his injured arm hurt and he winced and lifted his face from hers.

"Are you my girl again?" he asked.

"Always, Kurt. I'll always be your girl."

He took his class ring off and put it on her finger. She gave him hers and he worked it onto his pinkie. They kissed again. Finally, Kurt put her from him.

"I've got to go now, Sweetheart."

Merrilee nodded.

They went into the kitchen hand in hand. Keith and Carla were still sitting at the table but Carla had turned so she was sitting astride Keith's legs. Her blouse was unbuttoned and his hands were busy inside it. He saw Kurt and Merrilee come in and looked quizzically at Kurt without detaching his lips from Carla's.

"For the love of mike, you two, show some class," Kurt said crossly.

Keith set Carla on her feet and stood up, grinning at his brother. Carla slowly buttoned her blouse, watching Kurt and Merrilee curiously.

"You all fixed up?" Keith asked.

"Yeah, I'm fine. Let's go."

"Come on, Carla," Keith said. "'Bye, Merrilee. Thanks for taking care of Kurt."

"You're welcome. Good night."

Keith and Carla went out to the car. Kurt and Merrilee kissed some more, clinging to one another tightly. They were both in a turmoil of emotions, confused and miserable and euphoric by turns. At last, Kurt tore himself away. Merrilee stood on the back step and watched as he got into the car and Keith backed down the driveway. Merrilee came running after them, the trash bag in her hand.

"Wait! Wait a minute, Keith!"

Keith stopped and he and Kurt stuck their heads out. "Yeah?"

Merrilee thrust the bag at Kurt. "Throw this away somewhere. I can't let my folks find it."

"Oh. Sure," Kurt agreed.

Merrilee handed him the bag and stepped back.

"Wait. What about your sweater, Merrilee? They'll wonder what happened to it."

Merrilee nodded. "I know. I'll think of something to tell them."

She gave him a radiant smile and went back to the house. Keith backed onto the street and drove away.

"Drop me off at home," Kurt said.

"You okay?" asked Keith.

"Just dandy. I'll take a couple of those pills the doc gave Dad for his back and go to bed."

"All right. I won't be late."

Kurt kept his cut from his folks, wearing long sleeved shirts and sweaters until it healed and trying not to give it away by the way he moved. It healed quickly and completely, although it left a scar, wide on his biceps, tapering to nothing just above his elbow.

As they had figured before they led the football team to revolt against the coach, neither the twins nor Jazzy had spots on any of the winter sports teams. That should have left them plenty of time for homework but they had other fish to fry.

Ashland is a small town in a lovely setting, climbing up the flank of Mt. Ashland in the Siskiyou Mountain Range. The founders had laid it out around a plaza and on three sides the business center radiated out from it. On the fourth side was an astonishingly large and beautiful park. There was a spring of lithia water and the pioneers had bottled it for the mineral water market in the early days. All that was left of the enterprise was a fountain of lithia water in the middle of the plaza and the name, Lithia

Park. Lithia water tastes nasty and leaves one in no doubt as to the reason the bottling plant failed.

The Kovaceks lived in an elderly stately home on Siskiyou Boulevard, a couple of blocks from the library, within easy walking distance of the park. Even after they acquired their car, the twins often walked to the park and up above the duck ponds and playground to the wilder, less frequented areas. One Saturday afternoon Jeb and Sam frisked around the three boys, ecstatic to be taken along to the park. It was a glorious, brisk day in late autumn and the boys and dogs were feeling the high spirits of youth. The park was full of families with shrieking toddlers and with college kids playing with frisbees. Avoiding the crowds, the boys climbed the hill above the Globe Theater where the Shakespearean company produced some of the Bard's plays every summer, and kept going up, paralleling the course of Ashland Creek as it sparkled along its way at the foot of the hill. They climbed steadily until they came to a clearing where they could sit on a log and look out over the park to the town below. They were far enough away that the traffic looked like mechanized toys in a Christmas village in a store window. The dogs were disgusted at the boys' stopping and raced away in a game of tag, the dry leaves crackling under their feet.

"You going home next weekend?" Kurt asked Jazzy.

"Yeah, the old man wants some help with that little skewbald gelding."

"We could come Sunday and help out," Keith suggested.

"That'd be good. I'm going Saturday morning, early."

The twins nodded and they sat silently for a few minutes, absorbing the peace and beauty around them.

"What do you guys think about college next year?" Keith asked. "Think you'll go?"

"I don't think so," Jazzy said. "I'll be going in with Dad on the ranch. No need for college to do that."

"I don't know," Kurt said. "Mom and Pop want us to pretty bad."

"What would your major be? Engineering?"

"I guess so. Are you still thinking about architecture?"

"That's what I'll take if I decide to go," Keith confirmed. "But..."

"But, hell, school's a drag," Kurt finished for him. "I'd about as soon do a hitch in the service."

"I've thought about that some, too," Jazzy said. "It'd be one way to get out and see some of the world."

Keith nodded. "I've been thinking about the navy."

"On the other hand," Kurt began.

Keith interrupted him. "On the other hand, there are lots of girls on campus and there aren't that many in the navy."

The boys laughed.

The sound of the dogs barking furiously came from some little distance.

"Oh, hell," Kurt said, "now what?"

"We'd better go see," said Keith jumping to his feet.

The boys went toward the sound of barking, calling the dogs as they went. The barking turned into a series of yelps and yips and the boys quickened their pace. Then there was silence. The boys called and the dogs finally came in sight. Jeb and Sam were both slinking, bellies low to the ground, tails drooping, whimpering softly.

Jazzy laughed and the twins began to swear.

"Skunked again," Keith exclaimed. "Don't you two idiots ever learn?"

Sam and Jeb cringed, tails wagging slowly and tongues lolling. Their body language made their apologies, acknowledged their culpability, and begged for absolution.

"All right," Kurt told them. "Come on, we'll have to scrub as much of that off as we can."

"You know," Keith added, "you'll have to stay outside until your perfume wears off."

The three boys spent the rest of the afternoon in the Kovaceks' back yard, filling a washtub with warm water and bathing the dogs, then drying them in front of an electric heater in the garage. They also borrowed their mother's blow dryer to speed the process along. When they were finished, Jeb and Sam were beautiful. But they still reeked of skunk.

The boys went inside and the dogs tried to follow them.

"Oh, no, you don't," Keith admonished them. "You guys stay out here in the yard until that smell goes away."

Jeb and Sam flopped down on the back step and looked on mournfully as the boys went in and closed the door.

"We'd better get cleaned up," Jazzy remarked.

Keith pulled a gallon of milk out of the refrigerator while Kurt checked the cookie jar. Finding it full of pecan sandies, they sat down at the kitchen table and wolfed cookies, drinking prodigious quantities of milk.

"Well," Kurt said, stretching luxuriously, "I'm going to shower and change. I hope that smell hasn't rubbed off on me."

"Who'd notice?" Keith asked innocently.

Kurt jumped up and tried to get a half-Nelson

on him but Keith evaded his grip. His chair tipped over as he got to his feet and grappled with his brother. Jazzy watched lazily until they banged into the table, upsetting a half full glass of milk.

"Hey, you guys, don't wreck your mom's kitchen." Jazzy scolded.

The twins immediately stopped wrestling and put the room to rights.

"Yeah, she'll be home soon to get dinner," Kurt remarked.

"I hope she doesn't let Jeb and Sam in when she comes," Keith said.

"She won't. She should be able to pick up that skunk aroma before she even gets out of the car," Kurt said.

"Dibs on the first shower," Keith called, racing up the stairs.

"Hey, I've got dibs on the first shower," Kurt hollered, racing up after him.

Jazzy shook his head, smiling a little, and went upstairs to his room.

CHAPTER 3

After dinner the boys cleaned up the table, loading the dishwasher and putting the leftovers away in the refrigerator, while Dextra supervised. Rudy was already in the living room looking for something watchable on TV. Dextra treasured the few minutes she and the boys spent in the kitchen after dinner. She didn't get to spend much time with them and this would be the last year she could claim them as her boys. After graduation in the spring, they would be young men, ready for independence. She only insisted that they help with the dinner dishes so she could be with them; it would really have been easier for her to do the chore herself.

She poured dishwashing powder into the dispenser cup, closed the door, and turned the switch on.

"I guess that's it, Mom," Kurt said, looking around.

"Looks like it," Dextra agreed. "Are you guys going out tonight?"

"Yeah. We may go to Medford to the movies or maybe we'll hang out at the mall," Keith said.

"Don't wait up," Kurt told her. "We may be late."

"Not too late," Dextra warned. "And for goodness' sake, don't get to drinking."

"No, ma'am," all three of them intoned.

"I mean it," she said sternly. "Jazzy, I'm counting on you to keep these two terrors on the straight and narrow."

"Yes, ma'am," Jazzy said with a grin. "I'll do my best."

"All right, go on, get out of here," Dextra said, smiling at them.

One by one they all three kissed her, grabbed their jackets off the hooks by the back door, and went out. Dextra yanked it open just as the latch caught. Jeb and Sam tried to sneak past her into the house but she shooed them back.

"No, you don't. You stink. Dogs that play with skunks can't expect to sleep in a nice warm house. You'll have to sleep in the garage tonight." She called to the boys, "And don't get any traffic tickets, no speeding tickets, not so much as a parking ticket."

"Yes, ma'am," they called back, laughing. "We'll be good."

Kurt stopped and turned to face her. "Awful good," he said solemnly.

"See that you are," Dextra said, smiling.

She shivered as she went back inside. It was cold and looked as if it might be clouding up. She was glad the boys had worn their warmest jackets, which were identical. That was unusual, their taste in styles and colors was normally quite different. She had dressed them alike when they were little boys but as soon as they got old enough to voice their opinions about such things, they had demanded differences in their clothes.

Keith backed the car down the driveway. "All right, where we going?"

"Not to the movies or the mall," Kurt said dryly.

"Let's switch those signs around," Jazzy suggested.

"That's a thought," Keith said, looking a question at Kurt.

Kurt nodded. "Let's do. I'm sick and tired of that stupid stop sign."

There was a certain intersection that the boys often used where a side road made a Y with the highway. A yield right of way sign would have been perfectly adequate for the intersection but the highway department, in its infinite wisdom, had put a stop sign there. Simple Simon found it very useful in keeping his production numbers up. There was another intersection out north of town, between Ashland and Talent, where two gravel roads intersected with only a yield sign. The boys had been planning to switch them for some time but had always found something more interesting to do.

"Are the nut drivers in the trunk?" Keith asked.

"Yeah, I put them there a couple of days ago, after I tightened those nuts on the delivery truck," Kurt said.

"I guess we'd better get the yield sign first," Keith said.

There was very little traffic at the intersection of the gravel roads at any time. At nearly eight o-clock on a Saturday evening in winter, there was none. Kurt and Jazzy took the sign off its post and put it in the trunk. Keith drove to the Y intersection. Switching signs there would be tricky because, while it wasn't a busy intersection, it did occasionally see some traffic. Keith stopped and Jazzy and Kurt jumped out and took the yield sign out of the trunk and laid it on the verge of the road. Keith parked a little distance from the sign so, if anyone came along, there would be no eyeball evidence connecting their car to the deed.

By the time he walked back to the signpost, Jazzy and Kurt had the nuts loosened. Lights approached on the highway and the boys hunkered down in the borrow pit. As soon as it was far enough past, they climbed out and took the stop sign off the post. Car lights on the main road caused them to hunker down and wish they'd waited until late at night to make the switch. But it was finally done and the yellow yield sign gleamed blandly in the moonlight. Keith went for the car then Kurt and Jazzy put the stop sign in the trunk. All the way out to the other intersection, the boys congratulated themselves on the wonderfulness of their ideas and the efficiency of their execution. It took just a few minutes to attach the stop sign to the post and get back on the road.

They drove aimlessly for a little while then decided to pick up Merrilee and Carla. Keith put his foot on the accelerator a little more firmly and the speedometer was up around 70 when the familiar lights and siren announced that Officer Simonson was on duty, alert and intrepid.

"Shit," Keith said. "I forgot about that barn. Damn the luck anyway."

"There ought to be a law against hiding like that," Jazzy said.

Keith pulled off on the shoulder and stopped, sighing resignedly.

"Pop's going to be mad as hell," Keith said. "It's not a month since I got a speeding ticket."

"Yeah, that was Simple Simon, too," Kurt said darkly.

Keith rolled his window down. "Yo, Officer, how's every little thing?"

Officer Simonson shown his flashlight around the interior of the car. "It would be the Kovacek twins. And Janowski, too. Must be my lucky day. Give me your license."

"You don't want to give me a ticket," Keith said with a charming smile. "I was only going about sixty or so. Give me a break, huh?"

"Give me the license."

"Come on," Kurt chimed in, "Kurt's still in hot water over that last one you gave him. You don't want to get him grounded, do you?"

"Is that a fact?" said the officer happily. "One more and they'll take your license away. Hand it over, Kurt."

"You give him yours, Keith," Keith said to Kurt. "Let's keep it evened out, that way we can both keep our licenses."

"Step out of the car, Kurt," Officer Simonson ordered.

Keith and Kurt got out, leaving the front doors open. Jazzy slipped out the far side rear door. The cop was busy with the twins and didn't notice Jazzy's movements; the twins did.

"You want to make sure he hasn't been drinking. If I were you, I'd put him through the test," Kurt advised.

Keith bulled up and took a swing at Kurt.

"Thanks a lot, Keith," said Keith.

Kurt dodged behind the cop and Keith lunged at his twin. They dodged back and forth, keeping the cop between them and facing away from his car.

"Come on, Kurt," Kurt wheedled, "you don't want Simple Simon to get a blot on his record, do you? He's only doing his job."

"Oh, all right," Keith said. "I suppose I'll have to do it. No telling who they'd put on this stretch if he messes up. How does it go?"

Keith balanced carefully on one foot, closed his eyes, spread his arms wide, and brought his index fingers in to touch his nose.

"Like this?" Keith asked, looking the epitome of good citizen cooperation.

"Kurt," barked Kurt, "quit playing games with the officer. Hand over your license. You mustn't keep this valiant upholder of law and order here. Why, he's got things to do and people to see. Villains to foil."

"I'm going to arrest the pair of you for obstructing justice if you don't give me that license right now," threatened Officer Simonson.

Out of the corner of his eye, Keith saw Jazzy lock the patrol car door and push it softly closed. Jazzy slipped back into the Kovaceks' car and sat watching the little drama as if he'd been engrossed in it all the time.

"Okay, I guess you've got me dead to rights this time," Keith said. He pulled his wallet out and began to berate his brother. "This isn't my wallet, Keith. You rat, you switched them again. If you've spent that twenty bucks I was saving..."

"I switched wallets! That's good," Kurt hurled back at him. "Man. I thought there might be something you wouldn't stoop..."

The cop interrupted wearily. "Save the crap, you guys. Nobody's impressed. Kurt, give me the damn license."

Glaring with mock suspicion at one another, Keith and Kurt exchanged wallets. Kurt went through Keith's, ostentatiously checking to see that everything was in order.

Keith took Kurt's license out and handed it to the cop. Simonson filled in some spaces on the citation form and handed it to Keith. Keith signed Kurt's name and accepted his copy and Kurt's license from the cop.

"Thank you, gentlemen," Officer Simonson said ironically. "Have a pleasant evening -- far away from my beat."

The cop walked back to his patrol car as Keith and Kurt got into their car. Jazzy was watching out the back window as Officer Simonson tried to open his car door and couldn't.

"Go, Keith," he said urgently. "Don't peel out but go now."

The cop bent over to peer through the door window, cupping his hands to see better. Jazzy began to laugh uproariously.

Keith pulled out onto the highway.

"What's up?" Kurt asked.

"Quick, turn here. We need to get out of here right now."

"What the hell did you do, Jazzy?" Keith demanded.

"I'll take the fifth on that. But I will say that Simple Simon's keys are in the ignition and all the doors are locked."

"Beautiful!" Keith exclaimed.

"You're a genius," Kurt said.

The boys decided that discretion was the better part of valor and that an orderly retreat should be the order of the day. Sooner or later, Officer Simonson would gain entrance to his patrol car and if he caught up with them that night there would be hell to pay. If they gave him a little time to cool off, he would realize that he had nothing that he could pin on them. Any lawyer would point out that he may very well have inadvertently locked the keys in himself and there was no way he could prove that he didn't. However, he and they knew the truth of the matter and that it amounted to a declaration of more or less open warfare.

It wasn't until the night before the Winter

Formal that they tangled with Officer Simonson again. They knew that he was looking for a chance to nail them for something and it had a nuisance value. For one thing, they had to keep their driving speed down almost to the legal limit, especially in the vicinity of the old barn. For another, they had to be very circumspect about drinking, which meant that they had to find a couple of new spots. Lithia Park ought to have been safe but they knew that Simple Simon would have enlisted the municipal cops to help him in his vendetta. So they'd had to go farther into the park, which was inconvenient, or up Mt. Ashland on one of the old dirt roads. His interference with their pursuit of happiness could not go without retaliation.

Lora came over from Fort Klamath the Friday afternoon before the dance to stay with Merrilee. Keith had broken up with Carla Springer and was dating Jackie Bartolini. The three couples were together in the twins' car when they put their latest plan into operation. Taking back roads, Kurt drove as near to the barn as he could and parked in a disused lane, behind a stack of hay bales. Leaving the girls in the car, the three boys advanced stealthily to the barn. Jazzy and Keith went along one side while Kurt crept along the other. A couple of nights earlier, they had attached a hasp to the doors. Jazzy carried a brand new padlock.

Through the cracks between the shrunken boards, they could make out the outline of the patrol car parked just inside the doors, nose pointing out, ready to leap into pursuit of any malefactors who might happen along. Keith and Kurt swung the doors closed and Jazzy snapped the padlock through the hasp. Gasping with suppressed laughter, they listened a moment to Officer Simonson as he jumped out of the patrol car and hammered on the doors, yelling impotent threats.

"Come on," Jazzy said. "He won't keep that up for long. He'll be radioing for help in a second."

The boys hurried to put the second part of their plan into action. About a quarter of a mile from the haystack where their car was parked, there was a dirt road, just a track, really, to allow the farmer access to his fields. It was so dry that the dust was deep and powdery. They figured that sooner or later Simple Simon or one of his brother officers would come down the road, looking for them. They crouched down in the shadow of a huge mound of blackberry vines to wait. In a few minutes they heard a siren and knew that help for the cop was on the way. The siren got louder and louder and then stopped. A few minutes later two sirens ruptured the silence of the night. One raced down the highway away from them, the other shrieked up the secondary road toward them. Quickly, the boys jumped up and scuffled their feet madly in the deep dust at the end of the access track. They retired back to their shadowy hiding place and enjoyed the spectacle of Simple Simon racing past the cloud of dust, slamming on his brakes, and backing up to drive into it. As soon as he was past, the boys ran for their own car.

The girls were in an agony of suspense, wondering what the sirens meant and if they were about to be arrested and sent to juvenile hall. Along with that picture was the picture of their parents and how on earth they were going to explain their descent into juvenile delinquency. When the boys got into the car, the girls bombarded them with questions, which the boys were laughing too hard to answer.

The girls demanded to know what had happened but the boys were intent on the final phase of their operation.

"Let's go," Kurt said. "Even Simple Simon will eventually begin to wonder why there was such a big dust cloud at the end of the track and none anywhere else."

"He'll be back this way any minute," Jazzy agreed.

Keith drove the car, without lights, slowly

over the pasture to the barn. He backed in as far as he could and killed the engine. Kurt broke out a case of beer and the boys told and retold how they made their great coup. The girls were wide-eyed with admiration and pleasurable excitement and apprehension. They drank beer and listened to the cop come racing back down the road onto the highway. They whooped and shouted and forgave Officer Simonson his sins against them in their jubilation over their own cleverness.

CHAPTER 4

The winter passed quite happily for Keith and Kurt, Jazzy and Lora. Merrilee was torn between her love for Kurt and her love for her parents but she submerged her pain when she and Kurt were together. Keith continued to play the field, carefully avoiding the "good" girls. The three boys loved to ski and spent what time and money they could on Mt. Shasta and Mt. Ashland. They even managed a couple of trips to the slopes of Mt. Batchelor up near Bend. There was work, too. They spent some evenings and most Saturdays helping out at the store, as they had since they'd been big enough. Now and then the twins would spend a weekend at the Janowski ranch.

During the annual false spring, when temperatures rise and the days are so balmy that the farmers are deceived into beginning to work the ground for planting, Kurt and Keith went home with Jazzy. Weldon Janowski was not a farmer but a rancher. He raised horses and cattle and put up great stacks of hay on some land he leased a few miles from his home place just out of Fort Klamath. Jazzy was the youngest of the three Janowski children and the only one who still lived at home. Wel and Marie were always glad when the twins came to visit because it seemed like the happy days when their children were home and they were all busy together.

Marie had the knack of making people feel at home. When the boys rolled in late Friday night, she had a substantial snack of homemade doughnuts ready. She went to the back door when she heard Jazzy's pickup drive in and opened it, waiting for them on the step. She was round-faced and round-bodied, with a smile that illuminated the sweetness of her personality.

"Come in, come in. It's good to see you, boys. Come right in and make yourselves at home."

They all grabbed their gear from the pickup bed and went to the house. Jazzy went in first, carrying a large laundry bag.

"Hi, Mom," he said, kissing her cheek and giving her a hug.

"I see you've brought your laundry. That ought to keep me out of mischief for a day or two. And I think your dad has chores enough to keep the three of you out of mischief, too."

"Hi, Marie," said Kurt, with a grin, and kissed her cheek as he went inside.

"My word, you two are better looking than ever. It must worry your poor parents to death," Marie said with a smile.

"Mom sent you this," Keith said, handing her a white pasteboard gift box, tied with a wide lavender ribbon. He kissed her on the cheek and closed the door as she went to put the box on the kitchen table.

"There was no need," Marie said rebukingly.

"Open it, Mom," urged Jazzy.

Wel came into the kitchen from the living room. He was stocky and carried himself with the grace of great physical strength and integrity of character. He shook hands with Keith and Kurt; he and Jazzy embraced.

Marie set out glasses and a jug of milk and took the cake cover off the plate of doughnuts.

"Sit down, boys," she said. "I know you're hungry -- I've never known you not to be."

They all sat down and helped themselves to doughnuts.

"You shouldn't have gone to all this trouble, Marie," Keith said. "Making the doughnuts yourself and all."

"I don't approve of store-bought doughnuts," she said. "They're all sugar and air, no nourishment at all."

The pile of doughnuts was rapidly dwindling, much to her satisfaction.

"They are sure enough the best doughnuts I've ever eaten," Kurt agreed.

"Open your present," Wel said. "Let's see what you've got."

"All right. I admit to curiosity myself," she smiled.

She carefully untied the ribbon and lifted the cover off. Astonished delight wreathed her face.

"Just look at this," she exclaimed. "Why it's simply lovely."

Marie took a tabletop fountain out of the box. It was large of its kind, tall enough to allow the water to fall a few inches. It was made of small slabs of opalescent petrified wood set about with chunks of rose quartz and amethyst crystals. At the foot of the waterfall was half a geode lined with thousands of tiny clear crystals that flashed like diamond points.

Wel got up to study it better. He looked it over from every angle, then pronounced. "I've never seen anything like it. It's wonderful. Where're you going to put it, M'rie?"

"I don't know. Somewhere I can see it lots," she said thoughtfully.

"Why not put it on the end table next to your chair?" Wel suggested.

Marie shook her head. "It needs to be against a wall."

"How about let's move that cedar chest Uncle

Ted made for you into the living room? We can put it against the wall between the two front windows." Jazzy offered.

"I believe that would look just about right," Marie agreed.

Wel nodded. "There's an outlet right there, too. You can empty the chest tomorrow and the boys can bring it down."

"Let's do it now," Keith said. "No time like the present. It's that chest under the window on the stair landing, I guess?"

"Yes, but I have to think where to put everything that's in the chest, first," Marie protested.

Kurt laughed. "What for? You've got three of the best furniture movers in the western hemisphere right here; and the strongest, too. We'll bring it down. Come on, you guys."

Keith and Kurt ran up the stairs while Jazzy and his parents went into the living room to clear the space between the windows. When the chest was in place, Marie brought the fountain in and centered it. Jazzy filled the water reservoir and Wel plugged the fountain in. The water fell over the lip of petrified wood and plunged into the pool below, tinkling and bubbling.

Marie was delighted with her gift and Wel grinned happily.

They were all up early Saturday morning to

get a good start on the day's work. Marie fed them an enormous breakfast of steak and eggs, biscuits and honey, with plenty of milk and tomato juice. The big job was repairing the fence on the hundred-acre hayfield on the leased land. Wel had the wire and tools ready in the barn, along with some new metal posts. They loaded the pickup and set out.

The first order of business was to remove the old rusted barbed wire. That was accomplished without much problem, bar a nip or two when the wire broke and snapped at them. Wel took on the job of rolling up the old wire, as it couldn't be left laying in the pasture. There was a knack to that, criss-crossing the strands as it was rolled to keep it compact so it didn't fan out like a malevolent Slinky. Keith dug out the posts too rusted to be of use and set the new posts while Kurt and Jazzy strung the new wire, clipping it securely to the metal posts.

Kurt had commented on the fact that the fence was only two strands of barbed wire, wondering that it would keep cattle and horses off the hayfield. "Two strands is enough," Wel had said. "Anytime you see three strands in this country, it's a government fence -- Forest Service or Bureau of Land Management. Government's the only one can afford a three-wire fence."

Marie brought their lunch out to them and

watched them with pleasure as they ate.

"Lora's coming over this afternoon," she said, with a twinkle in her eye. "To help me with dinner."

"Well, she's a pretty good cook, Mom," Jazzy said. "You can use some help, can't you?"

"Oh, yes," Marie agreed, still twinkling. "I can use the help. It's just that she never offered before."

Jazzy had no answer for that so Keith chimed in.

"I guess maybe she never worried much about Jazzy's nutritional needs before," he said with a straight face.

"You think maybe she's feeling kind of broody, Marie? Sort of like a hen with a nest full of eggs in the springtime?" Kurt asked.

Marie laughed. "That's exactly what I think, Kurt."

"What's wrong with that?" Jazzy demanded. "Anyway, what about Merrilee, Kurt? Seems like she's got the nesting instinct pretty bad, too."

"If you ask me, you're both going to be old married men before the year's out," Keith said, shaking his head sorrowfully.

"Nothing wrong with marriage," Wel stated. "Best thing I ever did was persuade my wife to marry me."

Marie cast him a look distilled of nearly thirty

years of the ups and downs of marriage. There were traces of many emotions in it but mostly it was a look of love.

"Did it take much persuasion?" Keith asked.

Marie grinned at him, then at her husband. "It took some. I wanted to go to college and he wanted to go to ranching."

"So we compromised," Wel said, with a smile. "Same way we've been compromising ever since."

The three boys looked at him quizzically.

"We did it her way," Wel said.

They all laughed and Marie began to gather up the remnants of lunch.

"Now let's do it my way," Wel continued, "and get to work on that fence. We can finish today if we get right at it."

They pulled on their gloves and picked up their tools.

"Dinner's at six," she called after them. "Try not to be too late."

They waved at her and called back various reassurances that they would be on time.

At dinner that night, for which the men were only slightly late, the talk turned to plans for the future, as it often does in the months just before high school graduation.

"I'd like to see you get out and see something of the world, Jazzy," Wel said. "Our life here is good and you'll probably want to come back to it -- I hope you will -- but at least a year or two of college would be good for you."

"Or even a couple of years in the Job Corps," Marie added. "Not that it would be my first choice for you, but I do agree that it would be good for you to broaden your horizons a little."

"Okay," Jazzy agreed, winking at Lora, "how about I take a couple of years and hitchhike around Europe? If I like it, I can take in Egypt and China and Brazil."

"In fact, the whole world," exclaimed Keith enthusiastically. "Yeah, I think that's a great idea. Maybe we can talk Mom and Dad into financing us, too, and Kurt and I'll go with you."

Marie smiled at them tolerantly. "What are your plans for after graduation, Lora?"

Lora smiled at her shyly. "Well, I'm planning to go over to Ashland. I think I'll major in education. I'd like to be a teacher like you."

"That's certainly flattering," Marie said.

"It's a job worth doing," Wel said. "Takes a lot out of you but watching M'rie all these years, I'd say it has its rewards, too."

"That it does. At least in the primary grades. I don't know much about the upper grades or high school. I've never taught any higher than third. First is my favorite, the children are so eager and so earnest."

"That's what I was thinking," Lora said.

"Are we ready for apple pie with vanilla ice cream?" Marie asked, beginning to stack plates and silverware.

There was a chorus of assents.

"You shouldn't have done all this cooking for us, Marie," Kurt said.

"I had help, you know, so it wasn't hard," she said, smiling at Lora.

Jazzy snorted. "You had help, all right. I saw the Mrs. Smith's freezer boxes, Mom."

Marie laughed. "I meant to hide those. Okay, you caught me; I didn't make the pies from scratch. I'm not too proud to use prepared foods if they're good. But Lora baked the pies and we made the ice cream from scratch."

"I've never tasted better ice cream than yours, M'rie."

"It's my grandmother's recipe," she said over her shoulder as she carried a stack of plates out to the kitchen.

Lora helped her clear the table and they brought in the pies, still warm from the oven, and the ice cream. The boys appeared to share Wel's opinion; there wasn't much left when they finished, except Marie and Lora's beaming smiles.

The boys finished up the chores Wel had lined out for them by early Sunday afternoon so the twins headed home. Jazzy went over to Lora's; he would drive back that evening.

Having worked hard and been good all weekend, Kurt and Keith were ripe for mischief as they started home. Having plenty of time they decided to swing around through Jacksonville. It had been one of the first settlements in southern Oregon and owed its founding to the discovery of gold in what was now the middle of town. Jacksonville was a pretty place, quaintly antique. Many of the old buildings were still in use and the heart of it looked much as it had in the mid-1800s.

"They're still shooting that movie, aren't they?" Keith asked.

"Yeah. I hear they've hauled in dirt to cover the street, put up hitching posts, the whole nine yards."

"Let's go look it over."

"Okay by me," Kurt said.

They went into Jacksonville past the old Court House, now a museum. The main business street was blocked off to vehicular traffic so Keith parked the car and they ambled over on foot. It was late afternoon and the movie folk were busy effacing all signs of the twentieth century and installing those of the nineteenth. There were a lot of boxes on the porch of the United States Hotel with various props peeping out. Parked in front of the hotel was a large wagon-looking thing painted with garish colors and patterns and with lots of upright pipes of various lengths. Never having seen anything like it before, the boys went over to examine it and see if they could guess what it was.

"Some kind of organ, it looks like," Keith said.

"This seems to be a boiler or something," Kurt remarked, pointing to a big metal tank.

They walked around it, stooped to look at the underside, got up close to see if they could discover the secrets of its use.

A young woman noticed them and sauntered over to get acquainted. Her dark brown hair was long and loose with just a touch of waviness; she was dressed in jeans with an Adam Ant t-shirt that fit her snugly. Kurt and Keith found her extremely attractive.

"Hi," she said, dividing a smile between them.

"Hi," they answered, nearly in unison.

"Looking over the set, huh? What do you think of what we've done to your town?"

"I would hardly have recognized it," Keith said.

"It's not really our town," Kurt offered. "We're from Ashland, just up the road."

"Oh, where they have that Shakespeare

Festival," the girl said. "One of my friends played there one summer."

"Really. Are you an actress?" Kurt asked politely.

"No, I'm just a gofer -- you know gofer some coffee, gofer a light, gofer a hammer. Jillie Decosta," she said, shaking hands with each of them.

"Keith Kovacek." Keith said and pointing at Kurt, added, "My brother, Kurt."

"I never would have guessed," Jillie laughed.

Kurt turned back to the strange-looking machine and asked her what it was. Before she could answer, a tall young man came striding toward them, frowning ferociously. He was far from handsome but was well built and moved like an athlete.

"Hey! You guys get away from that!" he ordered.

Kurt held his hands up, palms outward, fingers spread.

"Hey, no problem," he said pacifically.

"We just wondered what it was, is all," Keith explained.

"Ignorant yokels," the young man grumbled. "Go on, now, get out of here. Jillie, go get me some of that lightweight chain and the side-cutters. We've got to get these signs up this afternoon."

"You know," Kurt said quietly, "I believe we're still in the U.S. of A. And as far as I know, nobody has repealed the constitution. This is a public street."

Another man came over, young but with an air of command.

"What's the problem here, Kenny?" the man asked.

"No problem," Kenny answered. "Just a couple of star-struck locals. I'll get rid of them."

"I don't believe you will," Keith said.

Jillie grinned, having smarted considerably under Kenny's overbearing ways. The second man was turning away but at that he turned back to see how Kenny would handle the situation.

"Look, you guys," Kenny said, his voice offensively patronizing, his expression sneering. "This isn't a public street, it's a movie set. We've got a lot of expensive props and equipment and we can't have unauthorized people wandering around. So do yourselves a favor and go find a sandbox to play in."

"We're not actually doing anything to you or your expensive props and equipment, much as we'd like to," Keith said, packing a serious challenge into the last phrase.

"Would you, now?" Kenny asked, with theatrical weariness. "You local kids are all the same. Think you're bad. Well, before you do anything you'll be real sorry for, let me tell you that I am a black belt and Les is a Golden Gloves champion."

Jillie snickered and Kenny shot her a furious glance.

"Hey!" Les exclaimed, "Leave me out of this."

Kenny gave his colleague a nasty look.

Keith and Kurt looked the other two over appraisingly, looked at each other, and nodded.

"I'll tell you what," Kurt said reasonably. "Let's you and me trade some punches, Kenny. Just for the fun of it."

Kenny laughed. "Trade punches? That's pretty crude. Just about what I'd expect from the local yokels."

Les was leaning against one of the porch posts of the U.S. Hotel, watching developments interestedly.

"I don't blame you for being scared, Kenny," Keith interjected. "I've never known an Angeleno yet who could fight. You're all mouth."

"That's a fact," Kurt agreed.

Kurt had more to say but was interrupted by Kenny taking a swing at Keith. Keith saw it coming and blocked it, then landed a solid punch to Kenny's ribs. Jillie was thoroughly enjoying herself, taking satisfaction in every punch that

Kenny absorbed, grimacing when Keith was on the receiving end. Kurt was trying to figure out a way to get Les involved; he couldn't see any reason why Keith should have all the fun.

Jillie was keeping close to the action and Les called to her to move farther back, out of the way. She ignored him and zigged to the right just as Keith zagged to the left, bumping together. Keith was momentarily off balance so when he caught one at the point of the sternum, he went sprawling. Jillie was knocked off her feet when Keith fell against her on his way down. Incensed, Les ceased leaning against the post and advanced on Keith with fire in his eye. Kurt was helping Jillie to her feet as Keith scrambled to his. No sooner was Keith upright than Les clobbered him with a good one.

Kurt saw Jillie hop up on the hotel porch then barely had time to notify his body that the round had opened when Kenny pasted him one. He retaliated and out of the corner of his eye, he saw Keith grinning as he and Les squared off. There wasn't anything even remotely like martial arts about the fight, nor any ring science, either. It was just a plain old American fist fight. Several of the movie people dropped what they were doing and came over to watch, making bets and calling out advice.

They were fairly well matched but Keith got

a little advantage over Les and knocked him into the machine that had been the cause of the fight. A big burly man protested and shoved Les out into the street, well away from the machine. That gave Keith the breather he needed and he closed with Les again, landing two or three well-placed punches to the body. Then he shot a glance at Kurt, to see how his twin was making out, and Les slammed his fist into Keith's jaw. That enraged him and he got serious, concentrating on finding Les' weak spot so he could put him out.

Meantime, Kurt and Kenny were slugging it out, toe to toe, almost as if they were merely trading punches for the fun of it. Kurt's nose was bleeding and Kenny had a cut over his eye when the town constable came running, accompanied by the assistant director.

"Arrest those hooligans," the A.D. demanded.

"Okay, okay, you guys, break it up!" The constable meant well but it was beyond his power to stop the four combatants.

The A.D. continued to yell. "Arrest them. I demand that you arrest them."

Just then Keith clobbered Les in such a way that the Angeleno fell backwards into the A.D. who recoiled fastidiously. One of the by-standers grabbed Les and another held Keith. There was quite a little crowd around them, which surprised Keith, now that he had time to look at them. He shrugged himself loose from his captor and stood watching Kurt and Kenny.

"Hey, Kurt!" Keith shouted. "Here's the law. Time to go home."

Kurt turned his head to look at Keith and Kenny connected with his chin, right on the button. Kurt sat down hard and looked accusingly at his twin. Kenny stood over him, fists still balled, still belligerent.

"What the hell did you do that for, Keith?" Kurt demanded. "You know better than to holler at a man in the middle of a fight."

Keith gave his twin a hand and pulled him to his feet, with Kurt fondling his chin and moving his mandible experimentally.

"Sorry," Keith apologized. "But there's a lawman here who seems to want us to listen to him."

They turned their attention to the constable. Les mopped at the blood on his face with a handkerchief and Keith handed one to Kurt, who looked at him questioningly.

"You're bleeding," Keith explained. "From the nose."

Kurt wiped at his upper lip and then held the handkerchief to his nose.

"Look, I don't know what all this is about and I don't care, but we have a city ordinance against street fighting."

"Not really?" Kurt asked.

"Yes, really," the constable said sternly. He pulled a small leather-covered notebook out of his shirt pocket and flipped it open. "I want your names."

Les chimed in. "Oh, now, I don't think we need to go that far. This was just a friendly little sort of a game, you know."

"That's right," said Keith. "Just a game. Trading punches. You know, officer, you've probably done it yourself."

The constable looked at the A.D. "There doesn't seem to be any damage to your stuff," he said.

"No damage at all," Kenny said. "I'm sure the producer would much prefer not to get involved in a legal tangle of any kind."

At the mention of the producer, the A.D.'s outrage faded. "I guess not," he said.

"That's fine, then," Kurt said. "I reckon we'll head on home now."

He offered his hand to Kenny and they shook, grinning at each other, while Keith and Les also shook hands. Jillie came over and touched Keith's face where it was red and beginning to swell.

"Does it hurt?" she asked sympathetically.

"Nah. Not much." He smiled at her and she took his right hand, examining the skinned and bloody knuckles.

Les took hold of her arm and yanked her away.

A wail arose from the audience. "You mean it's over? Who won?"

The audience grumbled and several people insisted that the fight continue until the winners could be declared, else who would get the money they'd bet?

"There's a law against gambling in this town," the constable announced. "Any money that's been wagered will have to be confiscated."

"Call it a draw," Kurt advised and added, "and give the money to a worthy cause."

"Like drinks at the J-ville," called out someone in the audience.

"Now that's what I call a worthy cause," someone else agreed.

"Come on, break it up," the constable ordered. "Before I run you all in." The A.D. began to herd his people away, muttering and scolding. Keith and Kurt started walking toward their car.

Kurt turned around. "Hey! At least tell us what the hell that thing is."

Kenny turned around and grinned at him, instantly wishing he hadn't when the pain informed him that he had a split lip.

"It's a calliope!" Jillie hollered.

"Thanks." Kurt gave her a wave and he and Keith turned the corner.

CHAPTER 5

Dextra was just finishing the after dinner kitchen cleanup when the twins came in the back door. Sam and Jeb came running to greet them, tails wagging, tongues lolling. Dextra smiled as they greeted the dogs then gave an exclamation of concern and dismay as they straightened up and she got a good look at them.

"Good heavens! How many of them were there?"

The boys grinned at her.

"Now, Mom," Keith admonished, "don't get excited. We're okay."

"What about the other guys?" she asked dryly.

"They're okay, too," Kurt said cheerfully. "We're just a little bruised, nothing permanent."

"Do you want some supper? Your dad and I just finished. There's plenty left -- pork chops, mashed potatoes and gravy, green salad."

"Um, no thanks. I think I'll have some milk and grab a hot shower," Keith said.

"Yeah, sounds good," Kurt agreed.

Keith went to get the milk from the refrigerator while Kurt got glasses out of the cupboard. Rudy, hearing their voices, came into the kitchen.

"Well, what do the other guys look like?" he asked with a grin.

"Pretty much like us," Kurt said.

"Am I going to hear about this from any kind of official?" Rudy wanted to know.

"Nope. Just a little friendly scrimmage," Keith answered. "What's a calliope?"

"Calliope!" Dextra exclaimed. "What on earth has a calliope got to do with it?"

Keith and Kurt took turns explaining about the movie set and the calliope as they sipped their milk, sitting at the kitchen table. Dextra and Rudy were vastly entertained but shook their heads at the willfulness of their offspring.

"I swear, sometimes I'm sorry I let you guys hang around old Sid Blumenthal," Rudy said. "You seem to have picked up his belligerence without acquiring his skill."

"Mr. Blumenthal is a great old guy," Kurt protested. "Why, he was a sparring partner for Sonny Liston."

"He was a prize fighter himself, too, before that," Keith added.

"Your father is not disparaging Mr.

Blumenthal," Dextra said.

"That's right. I'm only wishing you'd learned some of his technique. Maybe you wouldn't get beat up so often."

Keith stood up, grimacing as his various battered body parts protested against moving. "You could be right, Dad. Maybe we should get Mr. Blumenthal to teach some of the finer points of fisticuffs."

They all laughed and the boys took their bruised and stiffened muscles upstairs.

One evening in early May the kids paid a visit to a place they considered one of the most beautiful in Oregon and thus on the earth. Lora had again spent the weekend with Merrilee and they all decided to have a picnic at Tubb Springs at the summit of the Greensprings. Keith was dating Evelyn Duckett, so there would be six of them. The boys ransacked the Kovacek kitchen for paper plates, plastic flatware, pickles, and so forth, then they stopped at the Groceteria on Siskiyou Boulevard and bought a prodigious lot of sandwich makings, chips, sodas, and marginally wholesome snack items.

The drive up the mountain was uneventful but hilarious. Evelyn hid her eyes every time they got to where the shoulder of the road ended with an abrupt, naked fall to the valley floor far below. The road had been built in pioneer times, first for wagons and stagecoaches, later improved for Model A Fords. It was narrow, steep, and swooped around scores of sharp curves. The kids were all a little relieved when the forest began and gave at least the illusion of safety from the sheer drop.

Their high spirits carried them through the unloading of the car and setting out the food. It was really too cold to picnic but they were dressed warmly and had their youth to make even the simplest outings adventurous. They carried their provisions to one of the picnic tables provided by the State of Oregon for their convenience. Although it was still bright daylight down in the valley, it was twilight under the towering Douglas firs and pines. As they ate, they gradually grew quiet, the immemorial spell of the forest working on them. By the time they finished eating, they spoke in near whispers when they spoke at all. The atmosphere was hushed, as in a sacred place.

"This is so beautiful," Jazzy said softly.

"So incredibly, worshipfully lovely," Merrilee agreed.

"I feel like that, too," Kurt said, taking her hand in his. "Only I don't know what to worship."

"God, of course," Evelyn said.

"Whose God?" Keith asked. "Odin? The

Great Spirit? Jehovah? Mother Nature? Pan?"

But he didn't ask cynically, he asked softly, quizzically, really needing to know.

"It doesn't matter what you call him," Lora said. "It only matters that you do call him."

They sat silently, absorbing the holiness that they felt all around them, not really thinking at all. It was a moment of solemn happiness, of feeling the connection of their own souls to a higher plane of life. It was a satisfying instant of deep emotion that they did not understand nor try to understand. It was enough to experience it. The cold finally brought them back to earth. Lora sighed and stirred and the others became aware of the fact that they were freezing. They packed up in near silence and got back in the car.

Keith got behind the wheel and the radio came raucously to life as he turned the ignition on. He switched it off and they drove quietly down the mountain, their headlights swinging out over emptiness as they rounded the curves. They talked of their hopes for the future, their dreams, the work they would like to do, the good they desired to accomplish. As long as they lived, none of the six ever forgot that picnic.

Jazzy and Kurt and Keith all had senioritis in quite a virulent form. They stayed high on life, on the knowledge that in a matter of weeks they would no longer be schoolboys but men. It was heady stuff, stepping out into the world, choosing a college or university, choosing a field of study, making a beginning at independence.

One afternoon in the gym after graduation rehearsal, Mr. Hansen and Mrs. Marable handed out caps and gowns. Kurt was waiting for his while Keith was in a group of students, trying on their mortarboards and laughing at each other. Miss Sweeney, a tiny woman, middle-aged and wise to most teenagers in general and the Kovacek twins in particular, approached Keith. She was looking very stern and business-like.

"Keith, if I don't get that English comp paper, you're not going to graduate," she threatened.

Kurt joined the group in time to hear what she said.

Both boys looked inhumanly angelic and helpful. Then they turned to look at one another accusingly. "Keith," they said.

Seeing what was coming, Miss Sweeney was irritated. "For goodness' sake. Can't you just hand in the paper for once?"

"Yes, ma'am, Miss Sweeney. I'll see that he gets it to you by tomorrow morning," Keith said. He turned to Kurt, "Keith, I'm surprised at you."

Kurt shook his head sorrowfully. "Miss Sweeney, he's trying to pull a fast one on you."

"I know," she said.

Keith was indignant. "I wouldn't do a thing

like that. You have my paper -- it was the one on the Borgia family, remember?"

"I'm not likely to forget that one," Miss Sweeney said sourly. "But Kurt turned it in."

"You plagiarized my paper?" Keith demanded, turning to Kurt.

"You can't plagiarize your own writing and I wrote it," Kurt asseverated.

"All right, all right," Miss Sweeney said. "You know I'm not going to keep you from graduating. Keep the Kovacek twins here another year? Not likely. I'll split the grade between you."

"You really shouldn't, you know. You're just encouraging Keith to be irresponsible," Keith said, sending a disapproving look at Kurt.

"Besides, it isn't fair to me to give him half my grade," Kurt said.

"You are both incorrigible," Miss Sweeney declared and left the gym. The boys did not see the twinkle in her eye or her little smile of enjoyment as the door clanged shut behind her.

It was just days before graduation that disaster struck. Late one Saturday afternoon of a lovely spring day, Kurt and Merrilee, with Keith and Jazzy, were strolling through the little menagerie in Lithia Park. Keith had had a whim to feed the deer. They had stopped at a little store and bought some apples, which Keith and Jazzy conscientiously cut up with their pocketknives.

Merrilee held out her hand with a piece of apple on it and one of the does stepped daintily over to her. She shyly sniffed at the apple then carefully lipped it from Merrilee's hand into her mouth. Merrilee marveled at the softness of the doe's muzzle and the beauty of her big, soft, dark eyes. A tiny spotted fawn she hadn't noticed got to his feet and tottered unsteadily to the doe. The doe looked around and licked the fawn, standing still so he could nurse. Merrilee burst into tears.

"What's wrong?" Kurt asked, astonished. "Did she bite you?"

Merrilee shook her head, weeping and unable to speak. Kurt put his arms around her, holding her close.

Keith and Jazzy came quickly to her, concerned and ready to do anything that would help.

"What's wrong, Merrilee?" asked Jazzy.

"What is it, Kurt?" Keith asked.

"I don't know."

Merrilee looked at them through her tears, feeling their love and concern. She shook her head and pulled Kurt down the path, through the family groups and little knots of students, toward the duck pond. Keith and Jazzy looked after them, puzzled and helpless.

Standing under a dogwood tree in full bloom,

Merrilee gave Kurt the news she had been carrying by herself for the past three months. Shaken and contrite, seeing his plans for college and a career in engineering falling in ruins, Kurt held her close.

"Don't cry, Merrilee," he said softly, his cheek against her hair. "It's going to be okay."

She pulled away from him, impatient with what she felt was his avoidance of reality. "How can it be okay when I'm going to have a baby and there's college to get through and I've still got another year of high school?"

"We'll manage. We'll get married right away. I can get a summer job with Jazzy's dad and my folks will help us with school."

"Oh, Kurt. I want to be your wife so much but I didn't want it to be like this."

"It's my fault, Sweetheart. But it's going to be okay."

Merrilee shook her head. "Everything is spoiled. My folks will kill me. Or disown me. And I wanted to be a teacher."

"You can be. It'll be a little harder but we can still do it. Listen, we'll go to Reno tomorrow and get married."

"Kurt..." she began, having several difficulties to point out.

Kurt swept them all away with a kiss.

"We'll be fine, Merrilee. You'll be the

prettiest little mother in the world."

Merrilee smiled tremulously. Kurt kissed her again. They made their plans for the next day, deciding to call Merrilee's parents from Reno, after they were married. In no way did they underestimate the fury of her mother, who had always objected to Kurt as being too wild for her daughter.

The next morning Merrilee left the house at the time she usually started for school. She was wearing her prettiest skirt and blouse. She retrieved the suitcase she'd hidden in the shrubbery the night before and waited for Kurt around the corner from her house. Kurt drove up, hopped out of the car and opened the door for her, handing her into the car as if she were a fragile and precious spun glass figurine. He tossed her suitcase into the trunk with his and kissed her gently.

To Merrilee's surprise, instead of driving straight up to Siskiyou Boulevard, he turned at the Plaza and drove into the park. Keith and Jazzy were waiting at the lower duck pond, watching a young matron and her two small children. The little boy and girl were throwing bread to the ducks, laughing and squealing, as the ducks eagerly snatched at the food, swimming around and jockeying for the best spot. The male mallards' feathers gleamed iridescently in the sun, vying with the tulips and daffodils for beauty. The two swans swam up, looking regal and proud. With their much bigger size and long necks, they easily outmaneuvered the ducks.

The children didn't like the swans, though, they weren't fun to watch so they withheld the bread and tried to shoo the swans away. At that, the swans waddled up onto the bank and tried to take the bread from the children's hands. They were as tall as the children, which was very frightening to them and their mother. One of the swans pecked the little boy and the children began to scream and sought refuge behind their mother but the swans followed them. The distraught woman was trying to take the bread from her offspring to give the swans but the children's fists were tightly closed.

Hearing and then seeing their dilemma, Jazzy and Keith went over and herded the swans back into the water. The swans hissed and flapped their wings and glared ill-temperedly, but finally bowed to superior size. The mother was profuse in her thanks and, to the boys' great relief, took her bellowing small fry across the wide lawn to the playground.

Keith and Jazzy watched the swans who were now gliding around the pond, looking haughty and disdainful of such inferior species as humans and ducks.

Kurt and Merrilee walked arm-in-arm up the short distance to the pond.

"Here she is," Kurt called.

Keith and Jazzy beamed, Merrilee blushed crimson, and Kurt smiled fatuously.

Keith took her in his arms and kissed her before she knew his intention.

Kurt watched quizzically, then, as the kiss lengthened, he protested. "Keith, she's my bride."

Keith let her go then and she went to stand with Kurt.

"You're going to have to watch out for Keith, Merrilee," Jazzy warned. "He'll be pretending to be your husband when Kurt's not looking."

"I can tell them apart," she said, smiling adoringly at Kurt.

"In the dark?" Jazzy asked.

Merrilee blushed again and hid her face against Kurt's shoulder.

"You're about the prettiest bride I ever saw," Keith said. "I've always wanted a sister, you know. If he ever gives you any static, you let me know and I'll straighten him out."

Kurt gave him a look and said they'd better be starting. The four of them walked to the Chevy and Jazzy gave her a kiss on the cheek.

"Be happy, Merrilee," he said.

She gave him a dazzling smile. "Jazzy, I

didn't know anyone could be as happy as I am right this minute."

She gave him a quick kiss on the cheek and got into the car. Kurt closed the door and went around to the driver's side. He started the car and rolled his window down.

"I'll let everyone know tonight where you two are," Keith said.

"Thanks. I'll do the same for you someday."

Kurt and Merrilee drove away and Keith and Jazzy got into Jazzy's pickup and drove to school where they were late for class and unrepentant.

CHAPTER 6

Kurt had decided to go over the Greensprings to Klamath Falls and pick up Highway 139 south to Susanville, then to take 395 to Reno. He had a somewhat superstitious feeling that a stop at Tubb Springs would be an auspicious beginning to their marriage. Merrilee would have agreed if he'd suggested going to Reno via the Milky Way and sliding down a moonbeam. The radio was playing a popular song when it happened. Never after, as long as she lived, could Merrilee bear to hear either the song or the singer.

They were making the long, crooked climb up the Greensprings with a nearly sheer drop on the off side when an on-coming car, traveling too fast and halfway over the line, smashed into them. Kurt slammed on the brakes as soon as he saw the danger but there was no time nor road to save them. Their car flew over the inadequate shoulder and flipped over. When it finally hit the ground it rolled over and over until a mistletoe-festooned oak tree caught it and held it.

Merrilee returned to consciousness slowly, reluctantly. She was lying on a wire basket stretcher and some men were putting her in an ambulance. There was another basket stretcher on the shoulder of the road, the body on it covered, even the face. Merrilee closed her eyes.

"Kurt?" she asked, her voice almost too faint for the ambulance attendants to hear. Getting no reaction, she opened her eyes and forced herself to speak louder. "Kurt. Where's Kurt?"

"Take it easy, miss," one of the attendants said. "We'll take care of you."

Merrilee looked farther out and was surprised to see several state police cars, red and blue lights flashing. One of the troopers was standing nearby. She called haltingly to him but he heard her and came over.

"Please. Officer. Please."

"Yes, miss?"

"Kurt...Where's Kurt?"

"Kurt's the boy who was driving with you?"

"Yes," Merrilee whispered.

One of the attendants shook his head warningly at the trooper but the anguish in the girl's eyes forced a truthful answer.

"I'm afraid he didn't make it, miss."

"No. No. No, no, no, no." Merrilee wanted to scream but the word came out in a whisper. Tears seeped from under her closed eyelids.

The men put her in the ambulance and closed the door.

The next few hours were forever after a blur when Merrilee thought of them. The next thing she could remember clearly, she was in the hospital and her mother was sitting beside the bed. Merrilee closed her eyes and braced herself for the onslaught. The door opened and her father came in, to stand next to her opposite his wife.

"She's conscious," Louise said, her thin, hard-featured face drawn into a censorious frown.

"Good," Nat said softly, picking up Merrilee's hand. Merrilee squeezed his fingers and looked up at him.

He was a gentle man, soft-spoken and kind. Merrilee had often wondered what brought her parents together, they were so different and seemed to have nothing in common. She was afraid of her mother's bitter tongue and had always depended on her father for moral support.

"Well, Merrilee, let's have it," her mother demanded. "What did you and that Kovacek boy think you were doing skipping school and running off like that?"

Merrilee closed her eyes again, her face reflecting only despair.

"For God's sake, Louise, this is no time for that." Nat gently stroked Merrilee's face.

"Is Kurt..." Merrilee couldn't bring herself to ask the question. "Where's Kurt?"

"He's dead," Louise said, with satisfaction.

"Louise! I won't have it. Either curb your tongue or get out."

Louise was astonished. Ordinarily her husband left her alone to say whatever she liked. She had long ago ceased to expect him to stand up to her. She rose to her feet and went to the door and through it without another word.

Merrilee was crying. She had known that Kurt was dead but somehow her mother's brutal statement, with the obvious satisfaction behind it, deepened the pain and sharpened it. Her father stood by her, holding her hand, feeling more helpless than he had ever felt in his life. When she calmed down a little and was capable of listening, he told her what the doctor had said about her own injuries.

She was in shock but there were no fractures and only a slight concussion. There were numerous bruises but nothing serious. She would not lose the baby. The irony of that started her laughing. She laughed and cried until her father began to think she was hysterical. He was just about to call for help when Dr. Jackson came into the room, eyeing her disapprovingly.

"Merrilee, stop that! You're scaring your poor old dad senseless."

Dr. Jackson had delivered Merrilee and had since treated her for everything from a sprained ankle to viral pneumonia. He stood beside her bed and frowned ominously.

"Stop it, I said!"

Merrilee struggled to regain her composure. Finally, she choked off her laughter and merely wept quietly.

"What set her off?" Dr. Jackson asked Nat.

"I was telling her what you said about her injuries and when I told her she wasn't going to lose the baby, she went berserk."

"Can you imagine?" Merrilee whispered. "Kurt is dead and I'm still alive. Still alive and still pregnant without a hope of getting married. An accident like that -- it killed the father but not the baby. I'd have thought the baby was more fragile than that."

"You mustn't think like that," Dr. Jackson said. "I want you to rest now and get some sleep. I want to keep an eye on you tonight but I think you can go home tomorrow morning."

The doctor had been taking her pulse and checking her eye responses as he talked. He patted her hand and nodded at Nat.

"She's going to be all right," the doctor said. "You go on and take Louise home. Come back about nine in the morning. I'll let you know then if she can go home. I think she can."

The doctor turned and walked tiredly out the door.

"Go to sleep now, honey," Nat said. "We'll be back in the morning and take you home."

"Okay, Daddy," Merrilee said in a small, bleak voice, trying to stop crying.

Nat leaned over and kissed her cheek. She clung to his hand then let him go.

Keith and Jazzy were in the twins' room playing a video game on the TV, Jeb and Sam lying nearby. The dogs had been strange the past couple of hours, especially Jeb. At intervals he pawed at Keith's knee and whimpered. Sam would lick his canine friend and look beseechingly up into Keith's face. Keith was puzzled by their behavior but merely patted them and told them everything was okay, whereupon they would make the circuit of the house restlessly, come back and repeat the whole performance. When the boys heard the doorbell ring, something in the quality of the ensuing silence made itself felt through their concentration in maneuvering the figures across the screen. Keith's uneasiness grew until he abandoned the game.

"Something's wrong," he said. "Come on."

He got to his feet and hurried down the stairs, Jazzy right behind him. Rudy and Dextra were standing in the foyer, wrapped in each other's arms. Hearing the boys coming down the stairs, they turned toward them and the boys' stomachs clenched apprehensively at the tragedy in their faces.

"Mom? Dad? What's wrong?" Keith asked.

He knew the answer, though. There was only one thing that could make his parents look like that.

"It's Kurt, isn't it?" Keith braced himself for the blow that was about to fall.

Dextra and Rudy nodded. Still holding onto each other, they reached out and pulled the boys into the circle of love and loss.

"Kurt's..." Dextra had to stop and gather her strength before she could continue.

"Dead," Keith said flatly. "He's dead, isn't he?"

"Yes, son," Rudy affirmed.

Stunned, incredulous, the four of them stood there, hanging onto each other desperately.

"No," Keith said. He said it very firmly, as if he could rescind the fact of death if he were only adamant enough.

It wasn't until the next morning, after a sleepless night, that Keith told his parents where Kurt and Merrilee had been going and why. They were sitting around the kitchen table, drinking coffee. Jazzy started to leave when he realized what Keith was saying but Dextra caught his hand and asked him to sit back down. The two families had always been close but he was extremely touched to be treated as a son in the most painful familial intimacy imaginable.

"Pregnant?" Dextra said the word as if it were from an unknown language. "Merrilee is pregnant?"

Keith nodded miserably.

"She and Kurt were on their way to get married?" Rudy asked.

Keith nodded. "Of course. Kurt loves -- loved -- Merrilee."

"Loves is right, son," Rudy said. "Present tense. Wherever he is now, Kurt still loves her."

"Okay," Keith yielded the point. "Now Merrilee's all alone."

"She has her parents," Dextra said.

"Her dad, maybe," Keith said. "But her mother -- well, you know what her mother's like. Mean as the devil. She's putting Merrilee through hell."

Dextra and Rudy exchanged glances. They did know the Corbins. Not well, but well enough to know that what Keith said was true.

"Have you talked to Merrilee?" Rudy asked.

Keith shook his head. "I went over there last night but Mrs. Corbin wouldn't talk to me. As soon as she saw who I was, she shut the door. Didn't say a word, just shot me a hateful stare and shut the door. But Jazzy talked to her dad." Keith smiled wanly.

"While Keith was at the front door, I knocked on the back door. Mr. Corbin told me Merrilee's in the hospital but they think she can come home this morning. She wasn't hurt bad, just a slight concussion and lots of bruises."

"Is she going to lose the baby?" Rudy asked.

"I don't know. He didn't say and I didn't ask," Jazzy answered.

"No, I suppose not," Dextra said. "I wonder if I should go over there?"

"Maybe we should both go," Rudy suggested.

"I guess so," Dextra agreed.

It was late afternoon when the Kovaceks returned from the Corbins'. Keith and Jazzy were in the living room, doing nothing, saying little. They looked up as the front door opened and searched Dextra's and Rudy's faces for clues to Merrilee's condition. Dextra and Rudy came into the room and sat on the sofa. Dextra's hand sought Rudy's and he held it, squeezing gently from time to time.

Dextra shook her head. "Louise wouldn't see us."

"Nat came to the door and talked for a minute but he said Louise was too upset to see anyone."

"I know what that means," Dextra said, angrily. "It means she hates us, just as she has always hated Kurt."

Rudy patted the hand he held.

"Did he say how Merrilee is?" Keith asked. "Is she okay?"

Rudy looked at his son, feeling his powerlessness to make things better. "Nat said she's all right -- just shock and a slight concussion. They had brought her home from the hospital and she was upstairs in bed."

Keith's need forced his father to continue. "She isn't going to lose the baby."

"Louise will probably force her to have an abortion," Dextra cried.

"Did Mr. Corbin say so?" Keith asked.

"No. Not in so many words. But his attitude made it clear that the baby is very much unwanted." Dextra began to cry.

"Well, honey, be reasonable," Rudy said. "If it was our daughter..."

"I know, I know." Dextra fumbled in her purse for tissues and wiped her eyes. Then her anguish found expression. "But it feels as if she's killing Kurt all over again!"

Rudy gathered her close to him and murmured meaninglessly that it would be all right. Keith knelt at her feet and she put her arms around him. Jazzy slipped out to the kitchen to make a pitcher of iced tea.

It would be years before Keith came to terms

with the loss of his twin. He managed to cope with the funeral and his parents' grief by refusing to acknowledge to himself that Kurt was really dead. Without ever putting it into words, even to himself, he pretended that Kurt had gone on an extended visit somewhere. In time, Kurt would come back and everything would be as before. Until then he, Keith, would humor their parents and friends and relations in their delusion. Rudy and Dextra found Jazzy a tower of strength. He seemed to know when to insulate them from the well-meaning ministrations of their friends and when to efface himself. He saw to many of the details of everyday life -- meals, housework, the mail. Keith tried to support his parents but he was too wounded to do much more than hug them wordlessly.

Friends came and made awkward little speeches of condolence, perfectly well aware that nothing but the passage of time can ease the pain of losing a child. They brought enough food to feed half the town. Relatives came and offered comfort through their own shock and grief. Wel and Marie Janowski came the day before the funeral, bringing Lora with them.

Dextra and Rudy clung to Wel and Marie, grateful for the good common sense of their oldest and closest friends. Together they went to the funeral home to choose a casket and make all the arrangements. Together they went that evening to look upon Kurt's face for the last time. Keith, Jazzy, and Lora went also. When they left, Keith was rigid with the effort to maintain his composure. Jazzy drove up and down the streets at random until Keith made a request.

"Lora, I need to know if Merrilee's coming tomorrow and they won't let me see her. Will you ask her?"

"Sure. I'll bet that witch of a mother of hers won't let her."

"She needs to be there," Jazzy said.

"Yes, she does," Lora agreed. "I think it would be better to go than to phone. Why don't you drop me off and pick me up in half an hour or so?"

"Okay. I'd offer to go with you," Jazzy said, "but I don't think they'd let me in, either."

"They may not let me in," Lora said. "But I think you're right, Keith, she needs to be there tomorrow."

The boys decided to wait for Lora in the pickup. They saw her go up the walk and ring the bell and then the door opened. Merrilee threw her arms around Lora and they saw Mrs. Corbin come up behind the girls. Then Mr. Corbin came and after a couple of minutes, the door closed. It was only about ten minutes later that Lora came out and climbed back in the pickup. Jazzy started up and pulled away from the curb.

"Oh, man," Lora said, "that woman is a piece of work!"

"What happened?" Jazzy asked.

"Merrilee opened the door and her mom came and tried to throw me out. But her dad came and told her mom to let us alone. It's awful in there. Poor Merrilee."

"Is she coming tomorrow?" Jazzy asked.

"Yes. Mr. Corbin said she could. He's going to bring her. I hope Mrs. Corbin doesn't come."

"I have to talk to Merrilee alone," Keith said. "Tomorrow, after the service, at the cemetery, I'll try to get Merrilee to come with me. You two watch and when you see us heading for the pickup, come quick and maybe we can get away."

"All right," Jazzy agreed.

"Okay," Lora said dubiously. "I hope we're not going to regret it."

"I'm sorry. I just have to talk to her," Keith pleaded.

Keith never remembered much about Kurt's funeral. The church was jammed with people but he was only vaguely aware of them. The minister spoke but Keith didn't hear him. He sat on one side of his mother with his father on her other side and the Janowskis and Lora next to them.

Merrilee sat with her parents, one on either side of her, at the back of the church.

Kurt was taken to the cemetery where his maternal grandparents and various other relatives were buried. It was an old cemetery, with tall mature trees giving it a feeling of peace and serenity. The trees closed out the sun so instead of grass, the ground was covered with the leaves of deciduous trees. There was one empty grave lot in the family plot so Kurt was laid to rest between his grandfather, whom he had loved, and his Great-aunt Tillie who had died before he was born. At the cemetery, sitting under the canopy, Keith kept himself under control, thinking of what he intended to say to Merrilee. He kept an eye on her, where she stood at the edge of the crowd, again between her parents. She was crying; her father had his arm around her but her mother stood stony-faced and implacable.

As soon as the minister crumbled the symbolic handful of dirt over the coffin, Keith rose and worked his way around to Merrilee. Lora went with him while Jazzy went to start his pickup. Lora went up to Merrilee and spoke to her. Merrilee turned to her and saw Keith a few paces back of her. She started toward him; her mother reached out to stop her but her father's hand shot out and gripped his wife's arm.

94

Lora went to the car and climbed in beside Jazzy. Merrilee and Keith talked a minute or two, then Keith went over to the Corbins.

"Merrilee and I need to talk," he said, glancing from Louise to Nat. "I know you hate me and would like it if Merrilee never spoke another word to a Kovacek, but we need to talk."

Louise's face reflected all her hate and anger. She started to speak but Nat squeezed her arm warningly. He nodded at Keith.

Keith turned and went to Merrilee.

"Come on, before your dad changes his mind."

Merrilee glanced back at her parents.

"They let me come with you?" she asked incredulously.

"Your dad did."

Keith opened the door of the pickup and Merrilee climbed in.

"Let's go, Jazzy," he said as he shut the door.

Jazzy pulled slowly away from the verge of the narrow cemetery road and on out to the highway.

CHAPTER 7

Jazzy drove out into the country and stopped at the edge of a pear orchard. He and Lora left Keith and Merrilee in the pickup and strolled down one of the rows. The trees were in full bloom, a canopy of fragrant white lace humming with the industry of the bees.

Merrilee sat looking at Keith, her face puffy with weeping, her blue eyes shadowed with pain.

"As I see it," Keith said, speaking gently, "there are only three choices. Abortion."

Merrilee flinched, as from an actual blow. She shook her head, searching his face for some sign of hope. "I can't," she whispered. "It would be like killing Kurt."

"I know. That leaves adoption or..." Keith paused.

"That's what my mom and dad want me to do. They want me to go away somewhere and have the baby and give him up for adoption and then get a G.E.D. and go to college the next semester. Maybe in McMinnville or Pendleton. Where people won't know about me."

"Is that what you want to do?"

"No." Merrilee was vehement. "I want to have this baby, Kurt's baby, and keep him and raise him. He's mine and Kurt's and no one should be able to take him away from me." She started to cry. "But how can I keep him, Keith? I don't have any money, nowhere to go. I can't raise him all by myself."

"That's the third choice, Merrilee." Keith smiled at her and took her hand reassuringly. "If you'll marry me we can keep the baby and raise him. There's no other way that you can keep the baby. He's a Kovacek and he's got to be raised a Kovacek."

"Marry you?" Merrilee was bewildered.

"I know it couldn't be a real marriage, Merrilee. I know you and Kurt were in love and I'm not asking you to love me or be a wife to me. I'm asking you to keep Kurt's baby from being born a bastard and given away to strangers."

"Keith, it's so good of you. But I can't ask you to sacrifice yourself for me. You've got plans for college and your own life. I can't ask you to give it all up for me."

"You're not asking me for anything, I'm asking you. Please, Merrilee. Let me take care of you and Kurt's baby."

"What about my parents? They'll never let me

marry you. You know how they are, especially my mother." Merrilee shuddered. "She's been so horrible ever since she found out."

"I know that. The only way we can do it is to go now. Right now. We can drive to Reno today and come back tomorrow. Wel and Marie will give me a job on the ranch for the summer and after that, we'll think of something."

"I'll have to stop at home and pack a bag," Merrilee said doubtfully.

Keith shook his head. "There's no time for that. We'll have to go now. Your parents may be home by now."

"I suppose they are," Merrilee agreed drearily.

Keith kept still, not wanting to pressure her into doing something she would regret but hoping she would see the rightness of marrying him. The silence stretched out into minutes. Finally, Merrilee took his hand and smiled at him. It was a tremulous smile, hampered by grief and fear, impelled by hope.

"Okay, Keith."

"Good girl," Keith said, patting her hand. "I'll get Jazzy and Lora and we'll start right now."

Keith and Jazzy traded off driving stints, taking the road south, through Weed, to avoid the Greensprings and its associations. They stopped at Hornbrook and called the four sets of parents, none of whom really understood why they were doing what they were doing. Lora's mother was afraid that she and Jazzy were eloping, too. She approved of Jazzy but wanted them to wait until Lora finished college to get married. The Janowskis and Kovaceks were together and were afraid the kids were setting themselves up for trouble. Seeing they couldn't be persuaded to come home, they urged caution and care and then sat around the kitchen table, drinking coffee and talking about Kurt, his many happy qualities and the dreams they'd dreamed for him.

Louise Corbin had railed at her daughter until Keith took the phone, told her goodbye, and placed the handset back on the hook.

They got back in the car, Merrilee nearly hysterical, and drove on.

"She said she disowned me," Merrilee sobbed. "She said I could never go home again."

Lora held her and patted her back, much as a mother with a small child.

"She didn't mean it," Lora said.

"Yes, she did. You don't know my mother. When she says a thing, she means it and she never changes her mind."

"Your dad will bring her around. Give her time."

"She wouldn't even let me talk to Daddy.

Daddy would understand."

"Your dad will get your mom to change her mind this time," Keith said.

"You don't know her," Merrilee said again. "You just don't know her."

She eventually cried herself into exhaustion and fell asleep. They stopped in Susanville and bought gas and coffee and doughnuts. It was very late when they got to Reno but, tired as they were, they were excited to be in the midst of the bright lights and the glamour of the forbidden. They drove up and down Virginia Street a few times, back and forth over the Truckee River bridge.

Keith had withdrawn several hundred dollars from his savings account but, not knowing how long it would have to last them, decided that extreme frugality was the order of the day. They found a motel on the outskirts of town and rented a room with two double beds, the girls in one, the guys in the other. They slept as tired and healthy youth can sleep, even in the midst of emotional trauma. Lora woke first and quietly as she could, showered and prepared for the day. She washed out Merrilee's and her own pantyhose and took them into the bedroom to dry over the back of a chair. The others were awake. Merrilee was morose and Keith was worried about her.

100

"Are you okay?" he asked, sitting on the side of her bed.

"Sure, I'm fine," she answered.

"Do you need anything?"

She smiled at that and he hastily added, "I mean, is there anything I can get you?"

"A toothbrush. I need to brush my teeth in the worst way."

"Don't we all." Lora said.

Keith stood up. "Jazzy, if you'll stay here with Merrilee, Lora and I'll go out and get toothbrushes and things. Okay, Lora?"

"Sure, I think that's a good idea," Jazzy said.

"Yeah, I'll go," Lora agreed.

Keith took a quick shower and he and Lora left. They drove around town, remembering how bright and cheerful it had looked the night before and seeing its tawdriness in the morning light. "The Biggest Little City in the World" was only a small town after all. They found a discount store and went in. Standing in the sundries aisle in front of the shelves of toothpaste, Keith tried to think of what else Merrilee might need.

"Do you know what kind of toothpaste Merrilee likes?" he asked Lora.

"Sure." Lora picked a small tube off the shelf and handed it to him.

He studied the pricing a minute, then put the small tube back and chose the large, economy tube of the same brand. "I've got to learn how to shop to get the biggest bang for the buck," he said with a grin.

"I guess you do," Lora said, looking at him with a mixture of surprise and respect. "You're taking this seriously, then."

"I've never been more serious in my life, Lora."

"Good for you, Keith. It isn't going to be easy but I think you can pull it off. Jazzy and I will help however we can."

"Thanks. It means a lot to me and to Merrilee, too, to have your friendship."

Lora was pleased and a little embarrassed by Keith's earnestness and began to busily pick out toothbrushes for them all.

"Should I get her a new dress to be married in?" Keith asked, as they picked up a carton of orange juice.

"No, I don't think so." Lora considered. "It would be too much like a wedding. I mean, we all know this is a marriage of convenience...I mean, it's not as if..."

Keith took pity on her. "I know what you mean. We're not in love and there's no sense in pretending that we are. You're right. I just want to do whatever will make it easier and better for Merrilee. Kurt wants me to do that."

Lora had always known and accepted that the

bond between Kurt and Keith was stronger than the usual bond between siblings. She supposed it was their twinship that had kept them so close and in tune with each other. But she was surprised at Keith's use of the present tense and Keith saw it.

He nodded. "He's still with me. I feel his presence and sometimes I catch his thoughts."

Lora accepted that. She had never received communications from the other side or the hereafter or the next plane, however one wanted to refer to it, but she had no doubt that such communications were possible and did happen with other people.

Surveying their basket on the way to the checkstand, Lora swerved to an aisle of socks, pantyhose, and underclothes.

"A new dress wouldn't be right, but I know she'll want clean panties." She sorted through the colors and sizes and chose a lacy white pair for Merrilee. "And so does the maid of honor." She chose a pair of neon pink for herself.

"Well, I guess the groom and the best man had better have some, too." Keith went to the section of men's underwear and chose brightly patterned boxers -- green and white stripes for himself, white with red lips for Jazzy -- carefully explaining to Lora which was for which.

"Pretty Jazzy," she laughed.

"Real Jazzy," he grinned.

After breakfast they checked out of the motel and set out to find a wedding chapel. They had all been a little apprehensive even though they'd always heard how easy it was to get married in Reno. In this case, they found the reality matched the myth -- it was astonishingly easy. The woman who greeted them at the door tried to sell them everything from a blue garter to an album of wedding photographs. Keith managed to avoid the major pitfalls but bought nosegays of silk flowers for Merrilee and Lora. The actual ceremony was so quick that Keith felt it was over before it had begun. A little dazed, he followed Jazzy and Lora back to the car, thinking that Merrilee seemed much more self-possessed than he felt.

The signs on the doors of the casinos warned them that twenty-one was the minimum age for entrance so, making various comments on the irony of a state that considered that gambling and drinking required more maturity than marriage, they filled the tank with gas and headed north. The closer to home they got, the more nervous and apprehensive Merrilee became.

Keith tried to comfort her. "I'll go in with you, Merrilee. You won't have to face them alone."

"Somehow, that's not a lot of comfort, Keith.

Not when you're the reason they're going to be furious with me. Especially Mother."

"Would you like for me to go with you?" Lora offered.

"No, thanks." She gave Keith a tiny smile. "My husband and I will have to go alone."

It was dark when Jazzy parked in front of the Corbins' house on Van Ness and, hand in hand, Keith and Merrilee went up the walk to the front door. It felt very strange to Merrilee to knock on the door to what had been her home only the day before. She stood on Keith's left side and held tightly to his arm with both hands. The etched eagle in the glass oval in the center of the door darkened and Merrilee braced herself. The door opened and her mother stood there, angry and implacable. She saw the wedding band on Merrilee's finger and her lips tightened.

"Are you and Keith married?" Louise demanded.

"Yes, Mother," Merrilee faltered.

"You're no daughter of mine."

Keith opened his mouth to protest this savage behavior but Louise closed the door with what sounded like finality to Keith and the crack of doom to Merrilee. They turned away and were down the steps to the sidewalk when the door opened behind them.

"Wait!" Nat Corbin came out of the house

and gathered Merrilee into his arms. "Merrilee, baby..."

Merrilee burst into tears while Keith stood by helplessly. Nat's eyes met his over the top of Merrilee's head.

"Baby, don't cry. Sweetheart, it's going to be all right," her father promised.

Merrilee laughed through her weeping. "That's funny," she gasped. "Oh, that's so funny! That's exactly what Kurt said. 'It's going to be all right.'"

Nat shook her gently then held her close again. "Don't, Merrilee, don't. Your mother will come around in time. Just give her a little space now."

"Time!" Merrilee choked on the word. "I'll give her time. She can have all eternity. I'll never bother her again."

Merrilee tore herself out of her father's arms and took refuge in the pickup. Nat turned to look at Keith.

"I know you are trying to help, Keith, but I think this was a big mistake. I wish you had talked it over with us first."

"I can understand your point of view, sir, but I have to do what I think is right. Merrilee is my responsibility now and I'll take care of her and the baby."

"How in the hell you expect to do that is

beyond me. Where are you going now, to your folks'?"

"Yes. We came here first so I don't know how they feel about all this but I think they'll let us in."

"I'll pack some clothes and bring them over. You'll be good enough to let me know where you are and how my girl is?"

"Of course. I'm sorry that Mrs. Corbin is taking it this way; it's pretty hard on Merrilee. I'm glad she still has you."

Nat offered his hand and Keith shook with him.

Their reception at Kovaceks' had no drama about it. They trooped into the kitchen through the back door to be greeted ecstatically by Jeb and Sam. The racket brought the Kovacek and Janowski parents and Lora and Jazzy. A round of hugging and kissing ensued but presently the women shooed the men into the living room while they fixed a meal. No one felt much like eating but Dextra and Marie thought it would cheer everyone up to sit together at the dining room table. Lora and Marie contrived to leave Dextra and Merrilee alone together while they went to set the table.

Dextra sat down at the kitchen table and took Merrilee by the hand.

"I have been looking forward to having a

daughter for quite a while now, Merrilee."

Merrilee looked down at their hands, clasped together on the table, and waited for a storm of reproach.

"It hasn't happened the way I thought it would," Dextra continued, "but you are very welcome to my family."

Merrilee's head came up and she looked her mother-in-law in the face. Gratitude overwhelmed her.

"I'm sorry, Mrs. Kovacek. I'm so sorry."

"Now, honey, stop being sorry. Nothing's to be gained by harping on the past. What's done is done and can't be undone. We must just set to work to make the best of everything. We'll talk about practical things tomorrow. For now, I just want you to know that Rudy and I are behind you and K..." her voice quavered as she began to say her dead son's name but she braced herself and continued, "Keith and there will be happier days."

In the living room, the men were already discussing practicalities. Jazzy had told his father that Keith wanted to work on the ranch for the summer and suggested that he and Merrilee could have the cottage on the old Hickman place.

"You could work for us at the store, you know," Rudy put in, a little hurt that Keith hadn't asked him.

"I know. I appreciate it, Dad. But Merrilee and I need to settle in together somewhere. If we stay here and live with you and Mom and work for you and Mom, we'll depend on you too much. I've got to take care of Merrilee and the baby myself. You understand."

Rudy did understand. Even in his disappointment, he was filled with pride in his son. Whatever else he was or wasn't, Keith was a man. He nodded. "Yes, I guess I understand."

"I expect we could drop in for a weekend now and then, couldn't we?"

"You know you can. Anytime."

Keith turned to Weldon. "What do you say, Wel?"

"I say I'm proud of you, boy. Sure, I have a job for you. It doesn't pay much and the hours are long and the work is hard -- you know all that. You and Merrilee can have the cottage, too."

"Thank you. When do you want me to start?"

"Day after tomorrow. That'll give you a day to get the cottage in shape -- no one's lived in it for a couple of years so it'll need cleaning -- and get moved in and settled. Jazzy'll pick you up at five and the two of you can start on that fence on the upper end of the big alfalfa field."

"You know how much I appreciate this, sir."

"It's what friends are for," Wel declared.

CHAPTER 8

Keith and Merrilee settled into the cottage, beginning what they would both forever consider the most surreal six months of their lives. They scrounged up a few sticks of furniture and bought a few necessary pieces at a thrift store. The cottage had two bedrooms and Merrilee and Keith each occupied one. Dextra and Marie were generous with linens and dishes and housewares, some of which neither Keith nor Merrilee understood the use of. Nat Corbin brought Merrilee's clothes to the Kovaceks' and had a long talk with his daughter. He left her with the assurance that he and her mother loved her very much and only wanted what was best for her. He also left her a check and urged her to call him if she needed anything. Later, when Merrilee unpacked, she found that he had sent her stuffed Snoopy, worn and draggled but still much beloved. Thereafter, she slept with Snoopy every night.

Keith worked hard that summer, leaving at

five every morning and sometimes not getting home until eight or nine in the evening. He had bought a second hand pickup as being the most practical vehicle for them at that point. Sometimes he drove it to work but usually Jazzy picked him up so Merrilee could use the pickup if she wanted to. But she didn't often go anywhere. As her figure thickened, she became more and more self-conscious and reluctant to go out among people, especially people she knew. Lora came to visit now and then but she was also busy with her own work and family obligations.

Merrilee determinedly kept the cottage spotless and in perfect order. Her cooking skills were rather erratic but she did her best to keep Keith well nourished. She cried a lot that summer, tears of grief, of anger, and of self-pity. She was angry with nearly everyone -- with Kurt for leaving her, with her mother for abandoning her, with her father for not taking a firmer stand with her mother, with society for turning her generosity to Kurt into an ugly and unforgiven penance, and with God for allowing it to happen to her. Sometimes she was even angry with Keith, though she tried never to show it. It wasn't fair that Keith should turn out to be some kind of hero to whom she must in all decency be grateful. She was grateful. But it wasn't fair that Keith, with his promiscuity and irresponsibility, had turned the tables on her and become absolutely monkish in his austerity and responsibility.

One evening when she was six months into her pregnancy, Keith decided to sketch her. He placed her on an ottoman and arranged a floor lamp to cast a soft glow over her. It was a hot evening and all the windows and doors were open to catch the crisp little mountain breeze blowing across an alfalfa field where the hay lay in windrows. The delicious smell of freshly cut alfalfa wafted through the room. Merrilee brought a cold can of beer for Keith where he sat at the dinette table with his sketch pad. She picked up the can that was sitting there and tilted it to see if it was empty. Keith gave her a quizzical smile.

"You're getting to be pathological about keeping the house neat. One empty beer can won't wreck it."

"I know. It's just that you're doing so much for me and all I can do in return is keep your house clean."

Keith took the can from her and set it back on the table, pointing to the ottoman.

"Sit back down, please."

Merrilee resumed her pose and Keith looked from his sketch to her and back again.

"Turn your head a little to your right."

Merrilee did so and Keith sketched busily. Presently, she arched her back and rubbed it with both hands.

Keith was instantly contrite. "You're tired. I'm sorry. I get excited and forget that you can't hold a pose forever."

"How's it coming?"

She went to look and Keith held the sketchbook out to her.

"I like it," he said.

"You're flattering me."

Keith grinned up at her. "You're a very beautiful little mother."

She picked up the two beer cans and Keith glanced at his watch.

"Nine-thirty. You'd better go to bed, get your rest."

She nodded. "You, too. Four-thirty comes awfully early in the morning."

"I'll say it does!"

It was toward the end of August that Merrilee began to feel sick. She didn't say anything to Keith at first, thinking it was nothing much and not wanting to worry him. Haying was in full swing and he was so tired when he came home at night that she didn't want to add to his burdens. He didn't notice for a day or two that she was droopy and had even less to say than usual. When he finally did notice, she told him she was feeling the heat a little but was okay. He looked her over anxiously and noticed that her hands and ankles were very swollen. She said she'd been eating corn chips and was retaining water, it was nothing to worry about. He tried to believe it but he was afraid it was more than that. He mentioned it to Jazzy that evening when Jazzy dropped him off.

"You want to start baling the little river field in the morning?" Keith asked.

"Yeah. Dad wants to get water on it as soon as he can. I'll come by for you as soon as the dew falls."

"Okay, but don't honk. Merrilee needs her sleep. She hasn't been feeling very well the last couple of days. I wish she'd see the doctor but she says she doesn't need to."

"Should I get Mom to come and see her?"

"I don't know. I made her promise to phone your mom if she feels worse. I guess not."

"Well, tell her to take it easy," Jazzy said.

"I will."

Keith shut the pickup door and went into the house as Jazzy drove away.

Merrilee wasn't in the living room and when he looked in the kitchen, Keith saw the breakfast dishes piled in the sink. That scared him. Merrilee never left a dish unwashed more than about ten seconds after it was used. He knocked on her bedroom door and went in without waiting for her to answer. She was lying on the bed, dressed but disheveled. She looked like a very sick girl in a great deal of pain. Keith gently sat down beside her and took her hand in his. Her finger bulged alarmingly on either side of her wedding band.

Merrilee tried to smile at him. "I'm sorry, Keith, I just couldn't fix your dinner tonight."

"You've got to see Dr. Bricker," he said. "I'm going to call him."

Merrilee began to cry. "I'll be all right."

Keith took her in his arms and rocked her, alarmed at how feverish she was. She clung to him, hiding her face against his shoulder.

"You said that yesterday," he reminded her. "You're not getting better."

He kissed her cheek and put her down. He went into the living room and picked up the phone. It was way past office hours and all he could do was leave a message with the answering service, asking the doctor to meet him and Merrilee at the emergency room. He went back to Merrilee.

"I'm going to take you to the hospital. I left a message for Dr. Bricker to meet us there but if he can't, you'll have to see someone else."

"Keith, I..."

Keith interrupted her. "I know you don't want

to. You have to. Is there anything you absolutely have to take with you?"

Merrilee shook her head and Keith picked her up.

"My shoes," she said, as he carried her out the front door.

"You won't need shoes. Not tonight anyway."

At the hospital he put Merrilee in a chair in the emergency room waiting area and went to explain what was needed. There were a number of other people waiting, some with the glassy-eyed look that told of many hours of diminishing hope and increasing misery. The woman at the admissions desk wouldn't even tell him if Dr. Bricker was in the building. She kept pushing a clipboard at him, insisting that he had to fill out the form before anything could be done. Keith gave her a look of incredulous surprise.

"What's the matter with you, lady? Get the doctor. Dr. Bricker. Dr. Gilbert Bricker."

The clerk responded with weary impatience. "Listen, that's not the way it's done. First, you fill out the form. You give me your insurance information. Then I take down the medical facts. Then I take your girlfriend back to wait for the doctor."

Keith leaned down and spoke through gritted teeth. "My wife. My wife needs to see a doctor and she needs to see him now."

The clerk got to her feet and gave him a condescending smile. "There are nine patients ahead of you. Your wife will wait her turn."

Keith didn't wait for the end of the sentence. He looked around, chose a door and quickly bounded through it. There were a number of people in scrubs, some busy, some chatting, one with his feet propped up on a stool, reading a tabloid article titled, "Science Proves the Devil Is an Extra-terrestrial from another Galaxy!"

"Is Dr. Bricker back here?" Keith asked politely.

A middle-aged woman hurried over to him. A pin on her green tunic proclaimed her an R.N. A small brass rectangle gave her name as Nannette Fasco.

"You'll have to go back out front, you're not allowed back here."

"I've got to have help right now. Dr. Bricker was supposed to meet us here. Is he here yet?"

"We'll call you when he's ready for you. Go back out front."

"What is wrong with all you people?" Keith was getting very, very angry. "My wife is sick, she needs help right now."

A uniformed security officer came through a door and paused to assess the situation. Nurse Fasco beckoned her over.

"What's the problem?" she asked. Her little

brass name plate proclaimed her to be Officer Doreen Graden.

Nurse Fasco shook her head. "Nothing much, just another eager beaver who thinks the rules don't apply to him."

"What is going on here?" Keith demanded. "My wife is sick. She needs medical attention. This is a hospital. You are supposed to provide medical attention but all you do is bitch about your damn rules."

Officer Graden took him by the elbow. "All right," she said, reasonably, "let's go out front and just talk this over sensibly and quietly. The quicker..."

Keith jerked away from her. "You people are unreal."

He spotted a door that opened into a corridor that seemed to lead toward the doctors' parking lot. He cast a glance of mingled fury and bewilderment at that segment of the medical profession in his immediate vicinity, rushed through the door, and sprinted down the corridor. Officer Graden raised her voice and ordered him to stop. He didn't bother to acknowledge that he heard her. He burst through the outside door and scanned the parking lot. The trouble was, he didn't know what kind of vehicle Dr. Bricker drove. Officer Graden dashed out the door and once more grabbed hold of his arm. She was talking high and fast but Keith had spotted Dr. Bricker walking across the parking lot and shook her off to hurry to meet him.

"Dr. Bricker," Keith called. "Thank God. Merrilee's..."

Officer Graden was in front of him, trying to tell him that he was under arrest for gross lack of reverence toward people in green scrubs and black uniforms or something. He put his hands on her shoulders and looked earnestly into her eyes.

"Lady," he said, "I don't have time for your games right now. The grownups are busy. Go play in the traffic or suck your thumb in the corner -- do whatever you want to but do it somewhere else. This is serious."

Dr. Bricker suppressed a grin and, taking advantage of the lull while she got herself under enough control to speak coherently, led Keith inside.

"What is it, son? Where is Merrilee?"

Keith explained Merrilee's symptoms as best he could. When they arrived at the command center of the E.R., Dr. Bricker began to bark orders and people in scrubs began to bustle around. Keith went out to get Merrilee, closely followed by the tabloid reader who had suddenly lost interest in the Devil's hometown. Keith got Merrilee into the wheel chair and walked beside her as the orderly pushed her.

From then on Keith's memory of that night was a dreadful montage of medical terms, the meanings of which he could only guess for the most part; scurrying people in green scrubs; Dr. Bricker looking grave; glimpses of Merrilee looking waxy and still; and Mr. & Mrs. Corbin. Much as he hated to do it, Keith knew it was only right to call Merrilee's parents. They had a right to know that their daughter was sick. After he talked to Nat Corbin, he called Jazzy. Marie answered the phone. She was shocked and blamed herself for not keeping a closer eye on Merrilee. She told him not to worry about the haying, Wel and Jazzy would make out all right.

He was sitting in a small room on an upper floor, waiting for Dr. Bricker to bring him news when the Corbins came in. Louise glared at him balefully but held her tongue. She sat down facing a window and stared out at the lights, ignoring both men. Nat went to Keith and shook his hand, thanking him for letting them know. Keith sat back down, nodding acknowledgement. The three of them sat in an uneasy silence until Dr. Bricker came in much later.

Keith and Nat rose and stood mutely, waiting for the doctor's pronouncement, knowing from his face that there was bad news.

"We did everything we could but we lost the

baby. Merrilee's going to be all right but she's got a long recovery ahead of her."

It's doubtful if any of them understood or even listened to Dr. Bricker's explanation of what had gone wrong and what he had done. All they really heard was that Merrilee would be all right. Louise got to her feet and approached the doctor.

"May I see her now?"

Dr. Bricker hesitated uneasily. "She asked me to tell you that she wants to wait until tomorrow to see you," he said after too long.

"You mean she said to keep me away from her," Louise said bitterly. "That's your doing, Keith. I'll never forgive you."

She turned back to the window.

Dr. Bricker shook his head sorrowfully. He turned to Keith. "She's asking for you, Keith. Go on in."

The doctor turned to go but Nat stopped him.

"The baby. Was it a boy or a girl?" he asked softly.

"A boy," Dr. Bricker said.

He went out, saddened that he hadn't been able to save the baby, grieved at the discord surrounding Merrilee.

Nat put his hand on Keith's arm.

"Don't take it so hard, Keith. Maybe it's all for the best."

Keith made a grab at his temper and succeeded in speaking softly and without passion. "I know you mean well, sir, but that's about the cruelest thing that's ever been said to me. This baby was my brother's son and your daughter's son. I don't understand how you can think it's for the best for him to be dead, too. Merrilee wanted this baby."

Louise flew out of her chair and confronted Keith, her face contorted with hatred.

"This baby had no right to be born. It brought shame and disgrace to Merrilee and to us. You and your brother have ruined my little girl's life."

Nat tried to shush her but she shook him off.

"But I'll get her back now," she exulted. "She'll build a good life with someone else. Someone worthy of her. I'm glad the baby's dead."

Keith set his jaw and turned on his heel. Nat remonstrated with his wife, Keith could hear him until he got to Merrilee's room and closed the door behind him.

"What's the matter with you?" Nat demanded. "Can't you see that Keith is doing everything he can to help Merrilee? He's hurting, too, Louise. And she's his wife. Don't ever forget that."

CHAPTER 9

Keith resolutely put the Corbins out of his mind and went to Merrilee. She was lying very still and wan. Her eyes opened when she heard Keith come in. He took her hand in his and stroked it tenderly.

"I can't seem to do anything right, can I?" she asked.

"I'm sorry, Merrilee."

"Keith, where are they?"

"I don't know." Keith had never thought of himself as religious but now he found that he did believe in a benevolent God who took the affairs of mankind to heart. "We have to believe that God is taking care of them."

"The baby is a boy. Did you know that?"

Keith took her in his arms, holding her tenderly, wishing he could shield her from the pain.

"That's what the doctor said."

"I killed them, Keith. If I'd been good, if I'd waited, God wouldn't have punished me by taking them."

"No, Merrilee. No. God isn't like that. He doesn't punish us by killing the people we love."

"My mother says He does."

"Your mother is -- mistaken. God is love. He isn't cruel and vengeful. Especially not to little mothers like you."

Merrilee began to cry softly. Keith put her down and took her hand in both of his.

"I wish I could believe that," she said. "God, I wish I could believe it."

"It's true. Believe it, Sweetheart, it's true."

"My little baby's dead. Such a tiny little thing. He was born alive, Keith. Did the doctor tell you that? He was born alive but he was too small. They wouldn't even let me hold him."

"It's okay, Merrilee. God and Kurt are taking care of him."

"Are they? Are Kurt and the baby together? Keith, if I could believe that, I could go on living."

"Of course they're together. God wouldn't let them be separated."

"I want to be with them, too. My baby needs his mother. I need Kurt. Why doesn't God take me, too?"

"I don't know. We just have to believe that He has a reason. Don't fight Him, Merrilee. Believe in His love and live because He wants you to."

A nurse entered the room, carrying a hypodermic syringe and a cotton ball. "The doctor has ordered a sedative, Mrs. Kovacek," she said, swabbing Merrilee's arm. "So you can sleep."

"Good," Keith said, watching the nurse inject her potion. "It's what you need, Sweetheart."

"Stay with me a little longer, Keith?"

"Of course." He pulled the visitor's chair up close to the bed and sat down, taking her hand.

"I'm sorry, you'll have to go now, Mr. Kovacek," the nurse said firmly. "Hospital rules."

"I'll go when she's asleep," Keith said.

"I'm afraid I'll have to insist."

Keith gave her a sweet smile and said softly, "I'll go when she's asleep."

The nurse frowned at him but decided not to make further issue of it. She left and Merrilee closed her eyes. When he was sure she was asleep, Keith let go of her hand and patted it softly. He leaned over and kissed her on the cheek.

To his surprise, his parents were waiting out in the corridor, looking worried and apprehensive. He gave them a tired smile.

"I might have known Marie would call you," he said.

"How is she?" Dextra asked.

"The doctor says she's going to make it but I guess she's pretty sick."

"The baby?" Rudy asked.

"We lost the baby," Keith said, his eyes filling with tears.

His parents enclosed him in a three-way embrace, murmuring endearments and tiny exclamations of dismay.

"Let's go down to the cafeteria where we can talk," Rudy suggested.

Downstairs, over cups of coffee that none of them particularly wanted, Keith told them what the doctor had said and gave them an abbreviated version of the Corbins' reactions.

"I wish you'd called us. We could have been here with you," Dextra said.

"There's no reason you should have had to shoulder all that by yourself," Rudy added.

Keith didn't say anything.

"Didn't you know we'd want to help if we could?" Dextra demanded.

"I know. Yeah, I know. But everything's been so sudden..." Keith trailed off, trying not to think about the last five or six hours.

Dextra patted his hand. "All right, we're here now. Tell us how we can help."

Keith gave her a ragged smile. "Just be good to Merrilee." He included his father in the smile.

"She's been through a hell of a rough time and her mother has been pretty terrible."

"Tonight? Louise was still angry with Merrilee?" Dextra shook her head wonderingly, unable to understand how a mother could withhold love and tenderness at such a time.

"Yeah. She thinks it's a good thing the baby died. Luckily, the doctor wouldn't let her see Merrilee tonight. I don't know what tomorrow will be like." He took a deep breath and stared into his coffee cup.

Rudy and Dextra looked at one another, reaffirming their trust in each other. They had weathered some bad times, the loss of their son being by far the worst.

"Did I tell you the baby was a boy?" Keith asked, looking up at them.

"A boy. A grandson. I'm sorry, Keith," Rudy said.

"They don't mean it, son," Dextra said. "Louise and Nat. Louise has always been hot tempered and she's still feeling hurt and angry. And we have to remember, no matter what has happened since, Kurt and Merrilee were in the wrong."

"Maybe so, Mom, but they weren't doing anything the rest of us weren't doing. It's pretty hard to see Merrilee suffer so much while everyone else goes scot-free."

Rudy surveyed his son with approval. It was a tough way to learn but evidently Keith had absorbed some important lessons in the past three months.

"I know this isn't the time to discuss it, Keith, but you might give it some thought, just keep it in the back of your mind, you know. If you decide to go to college in the fall, your mother and I will back you any way we can."

"Thanks. I'll finish the summer at Wel and Marie's, then we'll see. I don't know if Merrilee will want to stay with me or what."

"Don't decide anything in a hurry, Honey. Your dad and I are proud of you. Let's go home now and get some sleep."

Keith nodded wearily and followed his parents out of the cafeteria.

They didn't have an actual funeral for the baby, just a private service. Merrilee was still hospitalized so the only people at the service besides the minister were Keith and his parents and Nat Corbin. Jazzy and Lora and Marie and Wel had offered to come but Keith told them it wasn't necessary. He thought they seemed a little relieved.

He and Dextra had gone shopping together for a shroud. They settled on a tiny white christening gown, embroidered with lambs. When he saw the baby in the tiny coffin, dressed in the gown, he thought he had never seen anything as pathetically beautiful and never expected to again. He hoped never again.

A couple of days later, right after lunch time, as Keith was getting packed to go back to the cottage and back to work, the phone rang and he picked it up.

"Keith?" It was Merrilee, sounding flustered and upset.

"Yeah. Merrilee? What's wrong?"

"Can you come get me? They're releasing me from the hospital and Mother will be here in about an hour. But I have to talk to you first."

"Sure. I'm leaving now."

Keith found Merrilee thin and wan, waiting tensely in a wheelchair in her room. She had asked the orderly to give her flowers to other patients, maybe someone who didn't have any. Otherwise all she had was a small overnight bag and the purse her dad had brought her.

"Oh, Keith, thank God you're here. Please, let's go right now. We have to get out of here before my mother comes."

"Okay. Come on, Merrilee, take it easy, Honey."

Keith handed her the overnight bag and her purse and began to push the chair out into the corridor toward the elevators.

"Do we have to check you out or anything?"

he asked. "Aren't there some formalities involved here?"

"I don't know, I guess so. Only, please, hurry."

Keith stopped at the nurses' station and was told the doctor had released Mrs. Kovacek and everything was taken care of. Keith thanked his informant politely and, responding to the pleading in Merrilee's face, quickly wheeled her into the elevator and then out the front door.

"Now," he said, when they were in the pickup and he had pulled out of the hospital drive onto the street, "what is this all about? Why the big rush?"

"Thanks, Keith. I just had to get away from my mother one last time. Will you take me to the baby's grave? And to Kurt's?"

"Of course. You know I will."

"I don't even know where he is. My darling little baby. Mother won't let Daddy tell me anything and she won't tell me, either."

"We wanted to put him next to Kurt but there wasn't room. That cemetery is nearly filled, you know, but we found a lot not far away."

"Did you order the headstone? Did you tell them what to put on it, like I asked?"

Keith nodded. "'Kurt Keith, beloved son of Kurt and Merrilee Kovacek, born and died' and the date."

"That's right. It isn't a lie, Keith. Kurt and I did love our baby."

Keith gave her a sympathetic smile and patted her arm.

"Stop at a florist's, will you?"

Keith shot her a doubtful look but drove to one just off the highway. It had several greenhouses behind it and a thriving nursery department as well. Keith pulled into the parking lot and stopped, then went around to open the door for Merrilee. He started to go in with her but she stopped him, gazing up at him with eyes dark with pain.

"Let me go alone, Keith? I need to do this myself."

He nodded and propped himself against the fender of his pickup, watching her go inside. It wasn't long before she came out with two large sheaves of flowers, one of Shasta daisies and delphiniums, one of white baby roses, both with fern leaves and clouds of tiny white flowers. She insisted on holding them on the way to the cemetery.

She let Keith hold the baby roses while she went to Kurt's gave and placed the blue and white flowers on it. She knelt, praying, then sat back on her heels to talk to Kurt. She was crying softly when she rose and looked around for Keith. He took the sheaf of roses to her and showed her where her baby lay. He had intended to go back and wait for her at the pickup but she reached for his hand and held him there.

"I don't know what to say to him, Keith. They wouldn't let me see him or hold him. How did he look?"

Keith told her softly and gently how the baby looked in his little christening gown, how his hair was brown like hers, how Dextra had tucked a tiny fleecy lamb into the casket with him.

Merrilee dropped to her knees and laid the roses on the baby's grave. She touched the tiny white flowers that floated around the roses and looked up at Keith, trying to smile through her tears.

"They're called 'baby's breath,' Keith. Isn't that ironic? Baby's breath for a baby whose first breath was his last."

Keith pulled her to her feet and held her close to him. She wept with great racking sobs that he thought would surely tear her in two. He gave her a little shake, then held her tightly again.

"Merrilee, don't. For the love of God, Sweetheart, stop it."

"I'm sorry," she managed to say. "Oh, God, Keith, I'm so sorry."

He got her back to the pickup and drove up into the hills above Jacksonville. The narrow blacktop roads were lovely and practically deserted. He found a spot where a disused dirt lane joined the blacktop and stopped. Merrilee had stopped crying by that time and gave him a bleak smile.

"Keith?" Merrilee's voice was small and tentative. "What are you going to do now?"

"I don't know. A lot depends on how you feel. What you want to do."

"I think we'd better get divorced," she said, not wanting to hurt him but wanting to get her life back in some kind of order. "I mean, I love you, Keith, but I love you as Kurt's brother. As my brother, not as my husband. You know?"

Keith nodded. "I know. It's okay. We knew it was just to legitimize the baby. I'll always love you, Merrilee. As my sister and Kurt's wife. What are you going to do now?"

"I'll go back and live with my parents. Mother's ready to forgive me as long as we get divorced. And Daddy wants me to finish high school this year and go to college next year. I guess I will."

"Me, too. Mom's got some admissions forms to fill out for Oregon State. It makes sense."

Merrilee took her wedding band off and handed it to him.

"Keep it, please. It's the one Kurt bought for you. It was in his pocket. There's an inscription."

She held the ring up to catch the light so she

could read the inscription inside the band. "You are my love, my life," she read. "Why didn't you tell me?"

"I couldn't talk about it and I didn't think you could, either."

She nodded her understanding, fighting hard to keep the tears back.

"If you ever need me, I'll always be there for you," he said.

"I know. You've been so good to me. I couldn't have made it without you," Merrilee told him.

"Yeah, you could. You're stronger than you think," he answered.

CHAPTER 10

When Keith graduated from Oregon State, he went to work for an architectural firm in California. He hated Long Beach; it was virtually a continuation of Los Angeles and he found everything about it from the climate to the overcrowding insupportable. He toughed it out for two years then went back to Ashland and opened an office a few blocks from Rudy and Dextra's office supply store. He had no desire to design skyscrapers or public buildings that would astonish his colleagues. Keith's interest was in buildings on a human scale -- useful, comfortable, and suitable to the site.

His brief marriage to Merrilee had made him realize that life exacted certain responsibilities. He became very serious minded after she divorced him and he took very little part or interest in the partying aspects of college life or, later, singles bars. Though he was far from appreciating celibacy, Keith began to see the sense in developing relationships.

One afternoon at the country club, after he had played eighteen holes of golf with a client -- he found that a great deal of his business was done on the golf course -- they had gone into the bar for a drink afterwards. Phyllis Rowe was sitting at a table near the big window with Roger and Marcia Otis, whom he knew slightly.

Glenn Logan, a roundish kind of man who combined a cherubic baby-face with an incisive mind, and Keith sat at the bar and talked about the hotel Logan was planning to build near the Plaza in downtown Ashland. It would be upscale accommodations for the Shakespeare crowd and Logan wanted to include some shops and a couple of restaurants, as well as a bar and spa. Keith had talked him out of building it in ersatz Tudor style -- the idea of a half-timbered ten-story hotel gave him nightmares -- and was now discussing the merits of including a conference center with meeting rooms in addition to a ballroom. He was not so engrossed in the discussion that he failed to notice Phyllis.

Phyllis was a small woman, her eyes were blue and she wore her light brown hair in a gamine cut. She sparkled with personality and had a sweet-toned laugh. Intrigued, he invented an appointment to cut short his discussion with Logan and stopped at her table as he left the bar. Knowing Roger and Marcia Otis, however slightly, gave him an excuse. Roger stood up and shook hands, inviting him to join them. He demurred, citing his imaginary appointment, and greeted Marcia. When Marcia introduced him to Phyllis, he was inordinately pleased to see that she was interested in him. He chatted only long enough to find out where Phyllis worked, then went back to his office.

Phyllis had a little dead-end job as receptionist/bookkeeper/secretary with Dr. Rodney Payne, a dentist whose office was in a newish professional building at the north end of Main Street, across from the George A. Briscoe Elementary School. Her professional outlook was not promising; she earned exactly enough to support herself and make it possible for her to continue going to work. She hated her job. The sound of the drill, the necessity of calling people to remind them it was time to come in for a checkup – she detested the whole damn job.

Two months after they met, Keith and Phyllis were married. Keith's mom and dad hadn't taken to Phyllis as much as Keith had expected them to but they tried to be happy for him. Phyllis had no family locally; she had been born in Kansas City and raised all over the map. Her father was about to retire from the Air Force and her mother lived in Austin, Texas with her fourth husband. Neither of them came to the wedding. Phyllis had been willing to go to Reno but Keith had insisted on being married in his parents' church. The associations with Reno were too painful.

They couldn't afford to build their dream house so they bought a craftsman style home on Gresham Street, up the hill from the library. It was a big pleasant house, the front yard shaded by a mature alder tree and the back yard by a copse of hawthorn and crabapple trees. Flowering shrubs were set against the fence and gave the back yard the illusion of being a room with living walls and carpet and a skylight of infinite proportions. Phyllis quit her job and devoted herself to making a home.

Keith turned one of the bedrooms upstairs into a studio and did much of his work there. He and Phyllis were in love and showed it so plainly that their friends kidded them about being joined at the hip. They enjoyed living together and they talked of every topic that came under their notice, they laughed, and they made love. Both of them wanted children; Keith passionately wanted a son.

They had been married fourteen months when Lindsay was born. Keith had a few pangs of disappointment at first, then fell in love with his daughter. She seemed full of magic to him -- he doted on her every burble. Lindsay was a starry-eyed baby, alert and interested in her little world from her infancy.

Jeb and Sam were gone by then, old age had claimed both dogs while Keith was in college, so he came home one day with a fluffy little black and white butterball of a puppy. He wanted to name her "Critter," but Phyllis vetoed that in favor of "Pepper." The puppy was a border collie mixed with cocker spaniel and the only thing cuter was Lindsay, who was a year old and just beginning to pull herself up and toddle around. Both babies were adorable, together they were irresistible.

Dextra and Rudy didn't even pretend that they were not completely silly about Lindsay and sometimes bought tickets to concerts to get Keith and Phyllis to go out so they could babysit. They had planned to sell the store and spend their winters in Arizona or New Mexico but with Lindsay's advent, they postponed retirement, wanting to be where they could spend time with her. After raising twin boys, they were enchanted with their baby girl. Dextra kept a steady stream of tiny frilly pink garments and baby accessories flowing into the nursery.

Keith's business went very well, right from the start. His work was original without being bizarre or impractical and he thoroughly enjoyed every phase of it. He hired Alicia Mathison, an architect who had just finished her training, to assist with some of his projects. He also hired a secretary to keep the office running smoothly. The only drawback was the demands of travel. He often had to be gone several days at a time, meeting with out-of-town clients or supervising construction. Phyllis objected strenuously to being left alone. She had traveled with him at first but with Lindsay's birth, she found travel too difficult. And she wouldn't leave Lindsay with Keith's parents for more than an afternoon or evening because they spoiled her so terribly.

Phyllis took great delight in her home and garden. It wasn't until Lindsay was three that she began to feel there were other interests in the world and that she was missing a great deal by spending almost all her time with Keith and Lindsay. At first it was merely a vague restlessness that she tried to ignore. She and Keith had never planned that Lindsay would be an only child but somehow she was not ready for another infant. Keith tried to be patient but he badly wanted a son.

One summer afternoon he came home a little early to find Phyllis in the kitchen washing vegetables, preparatory to dinner. She wore shorts with an abbreviated top and sandals. Keith found her delectable. Hearing the back screen door open, she turned her head to see him enter.

"Keith. I didn't hear the car."

He came up behind her and put his arms around her, kissing her neck. She smiled up at him and brushed her lips across his jaw.

"How far along is dinner, my love?"

"Thirty minutes or so. Hungry, huh?"

He let her go and went to the refrigerator to pour himself a glass of lemonade.

"Nope. I thought you might go for a little tennis and dinner out."

"Aren't you energetic at the end of the day?" she teased him.

Keith grinned at her. "I'm all revved up. The Wilkinson house is coming along so well it's got me all excited."

Phyllis turned off the water and dried her hands. "Is that all that's got you excited?"

He set his lemonade down and pulled her to him. "There are other ways of getting exercise."

She gently bit his earlobe. "Keep an eye on Lindsay while I go change."

He patted her on the derriere and she flashed him a smile as she went through the door to the hall. He put the vegetables in the refrigerator and went out the back door.

Lindsay was a little beauty. Her strawberry blond curls were the perfect foil for her dark brown eyes with their long black lashes. She was very busy with various plastic implements in the sandbox he had built for her under the hawthorn trees. Pepper was lying nearby but got up and pranced over to Keith as he sat down on the grass beside the sandbox. The dog bounced all around him, exuberant in her joy at seeing him. Keith patted her affectionately and Lindsay glanced at them tolerantly. Pepper raced off to find her ball.

"I'm making a house," Lindsay informed her daddy.

Pepper bounded back and dropped her bright blue ball beside Keith's right hand. He picked it up and threw it for her. She dashed after it and brought it back to him.

"I see." he said gravely to Lindsay.

She had made small mounds of sand and landscaped them with the blossoms of portulaca and violas. She had used sprigs of spirea and flowering almond for trees. She surveyed her work and reset one of her trees. He continued to play ball with Pepper while Lindsay gave him a tour of her house.

"The bedrooms are here," she explained, "'cause we get up early and that's where the sun shines first."

Keith was impressed. "Good. That's really good, Lindsay. You're getting to be quite a little architect. Hey, we'd better go in now. Mommy and I are going to play some tennis and you can watch and we'll go out for dinner afterwards.

How's that sound?"

"That sounds pretty fine. You and me better go change our clothes."

"That's exactly what you and me had better do."

He threw the ball one last time, telling Pepper that was all, and scooped Lindsay up and carried her into the house. They went to the park and played some tennis then drove to a buffet restaurant where Keith liked the fried chicken and Phyllis liked the salads. Lindsay followed her father's lead, demanding chicken with mashed potatoes and gravy and firmly disdaining any salad but red gelatin.

At home, Phyllis took Lindsay upstairs to get ready for bed. Keith showered while Phyllis bathed Lindsay then went downstairs and sat in his recliner chair, Pepper at his feet. He picked up his sketchpad and a soft lead pencil to sketch Lindsay in the sandbox with her house, the garden in full bloom making a lush and lovely background. In a few minutes Lindsay came toddling down the stairs wearing her pajamas and carrying a Little Golden Book.

"I'm ready for my story," she announced.

"Which one have you got tonight?"

"*Hiawatha.*"

Keith put his sketchpad aside and took her up on his lap. Pepper sat up and listened attentively, as if Lindsay hadn't "read" the book to her about a thousand times. Lindsay nestled against Keith and handed him the book.

"See, there's Tail-up-Straight and Short Hair. Short Hair's a baby bear. Tail-up-Straight's a squirrel."

"Sure enough," Keith agreed, suppressing a groan. "Okay, we've only read this one about forty-'leven times."

He smiled down at her and she gave serious attention to the book, just as if she had never heard it before.

"Close beside a big lake," Keith read, "stood a Chippewa Indian village. The Indians called the lake Gitchee Gumee -- the Big Sea Water. The water sparkled in the..."

Lindsay fell asleep at about the point when Nokomis was hiding the maple sugar from Short Hair but Keith knew from experience that if he stopped reading, she would waken and insist that he keep reading. So he read the rest of the book then carried her upstairs and put her in her bed. He put her favorite stuffed toy, a somewhat battered penguin, beside her and she put her arm around it. Keith leaned down and kissed her cheek, the poignancy of his love and tenderness causing his eyes to mist.

Leaving Lindsay's door open, Keith went downstairs to make his usual house-holder round, closing and locking doors and windows. Pepper followed him, knowing that her humans would soon be asleep and that she was charged with guard duty for the night. She sometimes slept in Lindsay's room and sometimes in the living room. She wakened several times each night and made a circuit of the house, checking for any signs of intrusion or danger.

Keith found his wife in the bathtub, immersed in bubbles, with half-a-dozen candles giving the only light in the room. Phyllis was lying back, relaxed. She opened her eyes and smiled at him. He pulled the vanity stool over and sat beside her.

"I've been thinking about our house," he said.

"Our house? Oh, our house."

"Yeah, our house. There's a piece of ground up Wagner Creek, back of Talent. About five acres. It's a beautiful site -- a view out over the valley, timber, the creek runs through it, high enough to be up out of the smog."

"It would be kind of a long commute."

Keith shook his head. "We'll build the studio next to the house and let Alicia and the draftsmen commute."

Phyllis smiled at him, at the way he had so taken for granted that he would have so much work that he would continue to need another architect and a couple of draftsmen to handle it all. He was so confident, so secure. "Of course. When can we start?"

Keith laughed delightedly. "There's a lot to do before we start building. For one thing, we haven't even bought the land yet."

She stepped out of the tub. He stood and swept her into his arms, carrying her into their bedroom. Later, lying together in the afterglow, Keith spoke softly.

"Let's make a baby."

"Now?" Phyllis kept her response light, not wanting to hurt him, not wanting him to know that she did not want another child. "Some guys are never satisfied."

"I'm serious, Phyl. We need a little brother for Lindsay."

"I don't know. I was sort of thinking about going back to work."

"Why? You don't need to. I'm not making millions but I'm doing okay. And it's not like you had a career to go back to."

Phyllis stirred irritably, pulling away from him. "I know. It's just...Sometimes I think I'm getting stagnant staying home all the time."

Keith was surprised. "I thought you were happy. I thought you wanted to take care of Lindsay and me."

"I do, Keith, I do." Phyllis began to feel a little panicky. "It isn't that. It's -- I don't know exactly what it is."

"If the housework is getting you down, we can hire someone to help out. Give you more time for yourself."

"I don't know if that's what I want."

"Maybe someone to come in a couple of times a week. You could get out with the girls, play some golf or tennis. Or maybe you could see if the Shakespeare Festival people need some help. You used to say you'd like to design costumes."

"Yes, but they don't want amateurs. They hire people with degrees, people with training in costume design."

"Go back to school, get a degree. I'll bet they have a program over at the college."

Phyllis could feel her irritation turning to anger but she didn't want to quarrel with Keith. She sighed. "I'll give it some thought."

Keith tried to decode the sigh, feeling that something inexplicable was going on in his wife's head.

"I have to go to Santa Cruz next week. Would you like to come with me?" he offered.

"How long will you be gone?"

"Eight or ten days. I'm not sure."

"I don't think so," Phyllis said. "It's so much easier to take care of Lindsay here than in a motel room."

"I wish you would. We used to have so much fun on those little trips. It gets pretty lonesome when I have to go alone."

"I know. But I'll pass on this one."

Phyllis turned her back to him and tried to go to sleep. An unreasonable resentment kept her awake. Keith should know what she wanted, she shouldn't have to keep explaining it to him. In her heart she knew that she had never explained her feelings to him and couldn't because she couldn't explain them to herself. That knowledge, nebulous as it was, only increased her resentment.

CHAPTER 11

Late that summer they began work on the dream house. Keith took Phyllis and Lindsay up to the site before they broke ground for the foundation and explained what they intended to build.

"We'll put a grass terrace here, so the garden and the house can blend together. This wall will be entirely of glass," Keith said, waving his arm to indicate the glass wall. "And we'll put a deck along the bedroom wing to overlook the valley."

Phyllis slowly turned in a circle, taking in the mixed forest behind and on the sides of the house site and the valley in front. "It's simply lovely. It'll be a wonderful home, Keith."

"Where will my sandbox be?" Lindsay demanded.

Keith picked her up and perched her on his shoulder.

"We'll make you a play-yard over here, Sweetheart. So you and Mommy can visit from the kitchen and living room."

Lindsay solemnly surveyed the spaces indicted by her daddy's sweeping gestures and pronounced approval. "That's pretty fine."

"Where will you build the studio?" Phyllis asked.

"Over here. The staff can have their parking lot out of sight of the house on that side and I can have my workroom on this side so I can be part of the home, too."

"It's so exciting. How soon can we start?" Phyllis took Keith's arm and smiled up at him.

He smiled down into her eyes and put his arm around her, holding her close. "I've got the ground sewed up so the well-driller will start Monday. I'll finish drawing up the plans when I get back from Santa Cruz. We'll be living here within a year."

Phyllis had given Keith's advice about getting out of the house now and then some serious thought. After he left for Santa Cruz, she called an acquaintance, Vi Devereaux, and suggested a round of golf. Vi was enthusiastic so they met at the country club and Phyllis rented a set of clubs. She was rather surprised to find that Vi had rented a golf cart. Phyllis was a little nervous at the first tee.

"Don't expect too much, Vi, I haven't played for years."

"It's not the game that matters, it's the

exercise," Vi drawled.

Phyllis laughed. "I see. No doubt that's why we use the golf cart instead of carrying the clubs and walking."

"Right. We don't want to overdo. Moderation," Vi said, winking at her. "That's the secret of life. Moderation in all things. Especially exercise."

Phyllis watched as Vi teed off. Her swing looked almost professional and she wondered if she would ever be able to play as well. In fact, she wondered if she would ever achieve Vi's insouciant manner and look of sophistication. Vi Devereaux was lean and lithe with a deep tan that came from a salon. Her impeccable grooming attested to many hours devoted to the various rites of the manicurist, hairdresser, masseuse, and personal trainer. To Phyllis, Vi seemed the epitome of feminine achievement.

After their nine holes, Phyllis and Vi sat at an umbrella table on the club house terrace with drinks in front of them. Roger Otis happened by and stopped for a moment.

"Phyllis," he exclaimed, surprised to see her there in the middle of a weekday. "Hi, Vi. Fancy meeting the two of you here. May I join you?"

Vi smiled cynically. "Hi, Roger. Certainly. I didn't know you two knew each other."

Roger moved a chair over next to Phyllis and

sat down.

"Yes, indeed," he said, smiling at Phyllis. "We've known each other for years and years, haven't we, Phyllis?"

"Well, maybe not years *and* years," Phyllis laughed. "But, yes, we've known each other quite a little while."

Roger put his hand over hers but Phyllis pulled away.

"I don't see as much of her as I'd like," Roger told Vi, "but we're old friends."

Phyllis was feeling just a little flustered, which caused Mrs. Otis' name to recede into the back of her mind. "How's your wife?" was the best she could do.

"Marcia's fine. She and Danny are visiting her mother for a couple of weeks."

"So you're batching, too," Vi said. "Keith is in Santa Cruz."

"We ought to get together and have dinner," Roger said to Phyllis. "Let them worry a little. Serve them right for leaving us alone."

"Why don't you? Teach them both a lesson." Vi suggested, getting what amusement she could from the situation. She hoped, of course, that more amusing developments would follow.

"I don't think so," Phyllis said uncertainly.

"There's Arlene Fore," Vi said, rising to her feet. "I need to talk to her. Excuse me."

Roger didn't succeed in getting Phyllis to have dinner with him that night but she had enjoyed the feeling of power that his importunities gave her. She had also enjoyed golf with Vi and drinks at the club house. She began to frequent the club, going out most afternoons. A few days later she was sitting by the pool in a swimsuit with an open beach wrap over it. She was sipping her frozen daiquiri when a hand lightly gripped her shoulder. She looked around to find Roger Otis smiling down at her. She smiled and indicated the chair next to her. He sat down and examined her with flattering thoroughness.

"You're looking quite exceptionally lovely today," he said.

"Thanks very much."

Phyllis knew, in her heart, how much such flattery was worth but she preferred to push the knowledge away and enjoy the flattery as if it were sincere.

"Marcia called last night. She's going to stay another week. Won't you take pity on a poor lonely man and have dinner with me tonight?"

Phyllis laughed. "I'm still alone, too. Keith won't be home for a couple more days. All right, you win. But just dinner. No dancing or nightclubbing."

"Of course. We'll go to the Ashland Springs.

No one could possibly read anything into two old friends having dinner at the hotel."

"No one could possibly notice two old friends there, with all the Shakespeare fans and tourists."

"If that's too crowded, we could try that place just this side of Grants Pass. I forget the name of it but I've heard it's very nice and the food is great."

He talked her into it and it didn't take an extraordinary amount of talking, either. Two nights later, while Phyllis was again out with Roger – she having justified it by noting that people have filthy minds but there is nothing wrong, in this day and age, with friends of opposite sexes merely having dinner together -- Keith came home to find Mrs. McAlister in his living room, watching TV. She was fiftyish, a white-haired motherly kind of woman, who helped out with the housework and babysat with Lindsay when Rudy and Dextra were unavailable. Keith set his suitcase down and Mrs. McAlister turned off the TV and rose to her feet.

"Mrs. Kovacek is out with friends."

"I see. Did she say what time she expected to be home?"

"No, she didn't. But now that you're here, I think I'll go on home."

Keith reached for his wallet. "How much do

we owe you?"

"That's all right," Mrs. McAlister said with a smile. "Mrs. Kovacek pays me for babysitting when she pays me for the housework."

"Okay. Good night, then. Thanks."

"You're welcome. Good night."

Keith held the door open for her and watched her down the front steps and into her car. She waved as she pulled away from the curb.

He left his suitcase in the entryway and went upstairs. Pepper met him at the top of the stairs, wagging her tail and whining and writhing with delight. He stooped to pet her and she rolled over to present her tummy, her tongue lolling. He gave her tummy a good rubbing and went to look in on Lindsay. He found her sound asleep, her arm around her penguin. He brushed his lips against her satiny cheek, marveling at the loving and protective emotions such a tiny little daughter could rouse in his parental heart. Pepper lay down on the rug beside Lindsay's bed, put her chin on her paws and prepared to keep watch.

Keith wandered into his workroom and stood looking at the preliminary sketches of the dream home. He disliked wasting space and building materials on hallways except as they served some definite need, beyond merely walls in which to place doors to rooms. He had managed to keep them to a minimum for the dream home but there was a tricky little convergence of walls where the master suite, living room, and study were situated. He didn't want to put a hall there but he didn't quite see how else to fit it all together. He picked up a sketchbook and pencil and took them into the bedroom. Then he showered and shaved and was sitting up in bed, doodling, hoping for inspiration, when he heard the front door open and shut. Phyllis came running up the stairs and stopped in the doorway to survey him, taking approving notice of his naked chest.

"Keith, I've missed you so much," she exclaimed.

"I couldn't stand being away from you for another moment so I drove straight through."

Then he had time only to toss the sketchpad and pencil on the floor before she whirled across the room and threw herself into his arms.

It always seemed to Keith that Phyllis was different after that trip of his to Santa Cruz. She was more patient and much calmer but her moods changed rapidly from droopy to weepy to sullen to merry to cheerful, in no particular order and for no reason that Keith could discern. He worried about her but kept it to himself when he found that it upset her for him to show concern.

He finalized the blueprints for the dream

house and work began on it. The well was a copious one and he began to think about the landscaping, now that he knew there would be plenty of water to grow whatever he liked, even in case of drought. He spent a lot of time at the site, supervising but also just enjoying the excitement of building a home for his family. The rocks for the big fireplace were delivered and dumped in a pile until they would be needed. Stacks of lumber of various sizes were delivered, along with pallets of pummy bricks for the foundation.

In the middle of all that excitement, Vi Devereaux gave a party. She and her husband owned a pretentious place up the Applegate River. The house was bastardized Italianate with a lawn that swept down from a wide balustraded terrace to the riverbank. Keith declared that the mere sight of that house on that site made him nauseous and that Vi Devereaux made him sick wherever he saw her. Phyllis coaxed him into going but she wasn't able to convince him that receiving an invitation was an honor.

Vi Devereaux greeted them with shrill little screams, liberally sprinkled with endearments. She brushed cheeks with Phyllis and gave Keith a hug. She kept her arm around his waist as she led them from the foyer into the living room. The music was too loud and too recent for the people she was playing it for. Keith couldn't see one person young enough to enjoy what he considered discordant racket. He was right, none of Vi's guests did enjoy it. In fact, Vi herself detested it. But it was necessary to her to project a youthful image and that meant playing up-to-date music.

"Come out on the terrace," Vi shrieked. "We're dancing out there."

As they passed through the room, Keith saw a four-piece combo in the wide alcove where Vi's grand piano lived. He was pleased at that because musicians, unlike machines, must stop now and then to recuperate from their exertions. That meant a few intervals of peace at any rate. Mercifully, someone came and detached Vi from him as they passed through the open glass doors to the terrace. He moved as far away from the band as he could get.

Keith and Phyllis nodded and smiled at the people they knew as they threaded their way through the dancers to the far end of the terrace. He leaned against the balustrade and watched the party. Phyllis stood next to him, smiling expectantly and a little wistfully. She was making little motions with her head and shoulders, keeping time to the music. He hoped she didn't expect him to dance. Not that he had anything against dancing but he insisted on

158

dancing to music and not to some cacophonous uproar with a beat so heavy he could actually feel it pounding on his ear drums. Then he got a delightful surprise. Merrilee Corbin was standing halfway across the terrace, smiling at him. She looked much the same as when they'd been married nearly fifteen years before. More mature, of course, and a little plump but still Kurt's lovely bride.

"There's Merrilee," he said. "Come and meet my first wife, Phyl."

He smiled at Merrilee and headed toward her. Roger Otis intercepted them and deftly detached Phyllis and danced away with her. Keith hardly registered the fact that they'd gone. Merrilee came to meet him and he swung her off the floor, spinning around a couple of times in his gladness at seeing her.

"Let me look at you, girl," he said, hugging her close and then stepping back so he could see her.

"Keith, oh, Keith," Merrilee burbled. "I didn't know how much I've missed you until just this minute."

They embraced again.

"How have you been, Merrilee? You look wonderful. Tell me everything." He looked around vaguely and added, "I seem to have lost my wife. Come out on the lawn where we can hear ourselves talk."

Vi had caused tiny white lights in vast profusion to grace the branches of the trees all around. It was about the only thing she had ever done that Keith approved of. He led Merrilee down the slope of the lawn to the edge of the water. The band was far enough away for their playing to sound more like music than caterwauling. They sat down on the grass and impulsively Merrilee reached out her hand to him. He took it and held it.

"Remember that night we all drove up to Tubb Springs?" Keith asked softly.

"I'll never forget it, Keith. It was so beautiful, so, I don't know, so touching some way." Merrilee drew a deep, ragged breath, and spoke shakily. "Let's don't go there, okay?"

"Okay. I just want to say that I've thought about it a lot through the years. It was truly a magical night."

"How are you Keith? Are you happy? I want you to be happy."

"I want to talk about you," he answered evasively. Are you still teaching?"

"Yes. I've been over in Idaho. Twin Falls. I've been teaching sixth grade but this coming year I'll be teaching fifth."

"Still in Twin Falls?"

Merrilee nodded. "I'm thinking of getting

married. Again."

Keith gently squeezed her hand. "It was a funny marriage, wasn't it? Do you realize that we only lived together for three months? I'll bet none of our friends would believe that we never slept together at all."

She smiled at him. "Who would expect one of the Kovacek twins to be such a gentleman?"

"It sure surprised me," he said.

"It didn't surprise me. You were marvelous that summer, Keith."

"I aims to please, ma'am. Tell me about this guy you're thinking of marrying. He can't be half good enough for you."

"He's a fine man, Keith. A few years older than we are. And he loves me. He must, I've kept him waiting for an answer for four years."

"Do you love him?" Keith demanded, thinking he heard a note of sadness in her voice.

"Not like I loved Kurt," she answered frankly. "I'll never love anyone like that again. But I care for him. I think I could be contented to live with him."

"Go for it, kid. Contentment is just as good as passion. Maybe better."

Merrilee heard the bewildered hurt in his voice and moved closer to him. He put his arm around her and they sat without speaking for a few moments.

"You're not happy, are you?" she asked. "What's wrong, Keith?"

"I was. Phyllis and I had something very special. She's changed, though. I don't know what caused it but something happened a few weeks ago when I took a trip to Santa Cruz. She wouldn't come with me and ever since then she's been different. I'm worried about her."

"I want you to be happy," Merrilee said earnestly, watching the reflection of the lights on the surface of the river as they glinted in the rippling water.

Keith kissed her temple.

"Maybe Phyllis and I can get back to where we were. I'm going to give it a hell of a try. For my sake, but for Lindsay's, too."

"Lindsay?"

"My daughter. Didn't I tell you about Lindsay?"

"No, you didn't. Tell me now, quickly. How old is she? Does she look like you? I'll bet she's pretty."

Keith laughed softly. "She's gorgeous. She looks a little like me and she's three. Think of all the superlatives that can be applied to a child and that's Lindsay."

"I have to meet her. When can we get together, Keith?"

"Anytime. Tomorrow?"

"Tomorrow. I'll call you in the morning."

"Great. We'll have a picnic in the park or something."

They lapsed into silence, punctuated by bursts of laughter from the terrace. Mercifully, the band was taking five or something. It was Keith who spoke first.

"What are you doing here? I wouldn't have thought these were your kind of people."

"Dad and Mr. Devereaux are business associates and Mother and Dad had to look in on the party so they talked me into coming along."

"You wouldn't have called me, would you?"

Merrilee shook her head. "It upsets Mother so much and that was such a painful part of my life. Not living with you, you know I don't mean that. I thought seeing you would bring back the pain. But it hasn't. It's reminded me how good you've always been and how much I love you. I won't be a stranger anymore."

"I'm glad of that. God, it's good to see you."

"Do you ever see Jazzy and Lora? Are they okay?"

"They lost their only child four or five years ago. He was only eighteen months old. There won't be any more. It broke them up pretty badly but they're dealing with it. And, of course, they have scads of relatives and always seem to have a bunch of kids around the place. They're okay."

"Maybe I'll stop in on my way home."

"They'd like that. I don't see them as often as I'd like. They're busy with the ranch and I'm out of town a lot on various jobs."

"I heard you were very successful. Are you satisfied with your work?"

"I guess we're never really satisfied with our work but it's coming along. I feel good about it. Phyllis and I have started to build our own home. Next time you're here I want to show it to you. There's not enough to show now."

"I'd like to see it." She reached up and ran her finger along his jaw. There was a catch in her voice when she spoke again. "You're so much like Kurt...I've got to go now. Dad's not very well and he wants to leave early."

Keith stood up and held out his hand to her. She let him pull her to her feet.

"Don't forget about tomorrow," Keith admonished her.

"I won't. I'll call you."

They walked up to the house and Merrilee went in search of her parents while Keith looked for Phyllis. The music was blaring again and Keith wanted nothing so much as to be allowed to go home. Phyllis had danced every dance with Roger but was not so absorbed in him that she failed to see Keith and Merrilee sitting on the grass on the riverbank. She had watched them come back across the lawn and up the steps to the terrace where they had kissed goodbye.

CHAPTER 12

The next Monday after Vi Devereaux' party, Keith spent most of the day at the dream house site, helping the crew pour the foundation footing. He was excited and happy, stripped to the waist, shoveling cement and sand into the mixer. The construction crew liked him and indulged him when it was his whim to help them. He was going to drive to Redding that afternoon and had asked Phyllis to pick him up, his car being in the shop. He would retrieve the car and be on his way no matter how much he longed to stay and work on his own house.

Phyllis was cold and sullen when she drove up and honked at him. He handed his shovel to one of the workmen and went over to the car.

"If you're going to leave by three," Phyllis said, without looking at him, "you'd better get started. It's one-thirty now."

Keith was hurt by her attitude but thought it best to ignore it.

"Thanks. Look," he enthused, "the

foundation's going in and as soon as it's set, we can start framing."

"Mmm-hmm." She still didn't look at him. "Is Alicia going with you?"

"No, not this trip. I've been thinking, Phyl. I think I'll ask Alicia to join me as a partner. She's a damn good architect and she's going to branch out on her own if I don't."

"Whatever you think," she answered disinterestedly.

"All right. I'll talk to her about it when I get back."

"How long are you going to be gone this time?" she asked, flicking a look at his face.

"A couple of days. It's just that little office building in Redding. But if the contractor doesn't get the masonry right, the whole thing will be a mess. I've got to go. Change your mind and come with me. We can get Mrs. McAlister to stay with Lindsay."

Phyllis rolled her eyes as if asking Heaven to enlighten her husband. "Are you coming or what?"

Keith's jaw tightened. He took a long drink from the insulated water keg, picked up his shirt and put it on, and got into the car.

That night, while he sat in a motel room in Redding, working on the specs for the masonry he'd come to supervise, Phyllis let Roger take her to a motel on the north side of Grants Pass, as far from Ashland and people who knew her as she could conveniently get. She had been technically faithful to her wedding vows until that night but she had known for weeks that it was going to come to this. She was excited and a little scared and underneath it all she was thoroughly disgusted with herself.

Two nights later when Keith came home from Redding, Phyllis was sitting with Lindsay on her lap, reading to her. Pepper was lying beside the chair. Keith had no sooner set his suitcase on the floor by the front door than Lindsay and Pepper flew out to him. Lindsay threw her arms around his knees and Pepper barked and danced excitedly around them.

"Daddy," she greeted him happily. "Daddy, Daddy, Daddy."

He scooped her up and she wrapped her little arms around his neck, pressing her cheek to his. He hugged her and carried her into the living room, Pepper frisking happily.

"All right," he said, in deep contentment, "this is a welcome worth leaving for."

He looked at Phyllis, uncertain of her response. She smiled at him and he relaxed. He set Lindsay down and went to kiss his wife.

Lindsay took the book from Phyllis and held it out to him. "You read me the story, Daddy."

"Let me catch my breath, Short Stuff."

He picked her up and stood her on the couch and rubbed the back of his neck, arching his back to get the kinks out after his drive. Pepper jumped up beside Lindsay, tail wagging at a rapid rate.

"Did you give your mother a hard time while I was gone?" he asked in mock severity.

Lindsay answered seriously, her eyes wide with conscious virtue. "Nope. I was good all the time. Real good."

"I bet," Keith replied.

He tickled her until she squealed and fell down on the couch, shrieking with laughter. Pepper nearly turned inside out with the delight of it all and Keith played with her as she jumped down from the couch and ran tight little circles around him. Having got both child and dog into a semi-hysterical over-stimulated condition, he had a job getting them calmed down again.

Later that night, after Keith had read Hiawatha to Lindsay and she was tucked in bed fast asleep, he and Phyllis went arm in arm into their bedroom. When he came out of the bathroom, the lights were off and the moon gave only a faint illumination. Keith had always liked to watch Phyllis' face when they made love so he switched on his bedside lamp. To his surprise, she reached across and turned it off. She was

169

very tender with him that night and he responded in kind. Afterwards, she lay with her head on his shoulder and he rejoiced in their closeness and the beauty of their love. Then he realized that she was crying.

"Tears? Why?"

"Keith, I've missed you so much."

"Now that I'm home is no time to cry."

"I know." She sat up and groped for a tissue on her bedside table. "It's just -- I don't know what it is -- I guess I need vitamins or something. I've been feeling so upset and out-of-sorts lately."

Keith sat up, grinning happily. "You're pregnant!" he exclaimed.

Phyllis laughed, not with amusement. "No. Sorry."

He pulled her back down to recline against him. "Okay. There's lots of time for you to change your mind."

"Lots of time?"

Keith was dismayed to hear an edge of bitterness in her voice.

"Lots of time?" she repeated, bursting into tears and sobbing. "If we've got to have another baby, let's do it now and get it over with."

"Phyl, don't, Honey. We don't have to have another baby. If you really don't want one, we won't. Of course not. It's just that I can't quite believe you really don't want a son as much as I do."

"I want to please you," she said, her sobbing quieting. "Give me some time, Keith. I'll try to get used to the idea."

"Have I made you feel like that? Forgive me, Sweetheart. I won't badger you anymore."

"Hold me. Hold me and never let me go."

She put her arm across his chest and pressed her face against his neck as he tightened his arm around her and kissed her hair.

Phyllis belonged to the PTA and a couple of ladies' clubs and, as a cover for her trysts with Roger, she told Keith that she had been appointed to several committees. He was very puzzled by her mood swings but was completely unsuspicious. One evening in the early fall, Keith and Lindsay were lying on the floor making designs with a compass and protractor. There was a fire in the fireplace with Pepper lying on the hearth rug and the picture should have been one of domestic bliss. But Phyllis was missing from the scene. Presently she came to the head of the stairs in her new coat. The color was very deceptive. In some lights it looked black, in others purple or blue. As she came down the stairs, pulling on her gloves, it shown iridescent, gleaming from color to color, sometimes seeming to be all colors at once.

"You're sure you don't mind, Darling?" she asked as she started down.

Keith watched and then gave vent to a prolonged wolf whistle. "You're gorgeous," he said. "No, I don't mind. You go on to your meeting, we'll be fine."

He got to his feet to kiss her goodbye but Lindsay hardly looked up.

"Goodnight, Lindsay. I'll see you in the morning."

Lindsay flicked her a look of irritation. "Goodnight. Me and Daddy are busy, so you better go now."

"Yes, sorry to keep you so long," Phyllis retorted, stung in spite of herself. She knew it was futile to be jealous of her own daughter and husband but it really bothered her that they seemed so content without her. And it hurt to the depths of her being when Lindsay made her little speeches, making it clear that she was Daddy's little girl.

"Drive carefully," Keith told her, as he always did when she left the house without him. "Enjoy yourself."

"I'll try," she said, waiting to smile until the door closed behind her.

As their affair gained momentum, Phyllis found that Roger depended on her more and more for emotional support. He had looked so strong and independent that she had thought she would be able to lean on him. Instead she found herself shoring up his sagging confidence. It was that boyishness of his that blinded her to the real dynamics of their relationship. She became more and more nervous and edgy, with her temper just short of flash point more often than not. Keith was at his wits' end what to do for her. Nothing he did pleased her and while she didn't neglect or mistreat Lindsay, it was evident that she had largely lost interest in the child. She still went through the motions of wifehood and motherhood but her performance was a hollow one.

She was cooking breakfast one morning when Keith wandered in and stood propped against the counter, sipping a cup of coffee and watching her. Her movements were sharp and quick and her mouth drooped unhappily. Pepper sat watching her, hoping it would soon be time for her breakfast. Phyllis wanted something from the cupboard where Pepper was sitting and yanked the door open against the dog.

"Pepper, will you get the hell out of here?" Phyllis stormed.

Pepper crept under the table in the breakfast nook, and looked sadly out at her people.

"It's been quite a while since you had a checkup, hasn't it, Darling?" Keith ventured at last, as she poured pancake batter onto the hot grill.

"Checkup?"

"Medical. Maybe you ought to let the doc look you over."

She slammed the bowl onto the counter where it broke into several large pieces, splattering pancake batter far and wide. She turned on him furiously.

"How the hell do you expect me to cook your damn breakfast with you standing there telling me I'm sick?"

"I didn't say that, Phyl." Keith was really alarmed at her overreaction. "I just think you're kind of short-tempered and it isn't like you. Maybe you do need to take vitamins or something. It wouldn't hurt to have the doctor check."

She tore a wad of paper towels off the roll and began to mop at the batter.

"I'm not going to the doctor and have him prescribe Valium so I can take this day after day. Like Marcia Otis. You'll have to find some other way."

"Some other way to what?"

Keith went to her and put his arms around her. She jerked away, throwing the messy paper towels in the sink. The pancakes on the grill began to burn and she yanked open a drawer to get a spatula to turn them with.

"I can't cook and screw both, Keith. If you want your breakfast get the hell out of the way."

He went out of the kitchen and started up the stairs for his briefcase. Phyllis came after him, carrying the pancake turner.

"Keith, don't go. Please don't go, Keith."

He turned slowly and looked at her uncertainly. She was crying. He held out his arms and she went to him, holding onto him tightly.

"I'll do anything you want," he said, stroking her hair. "But we can't go on like this much longer. What is it that's making you so unhappy? Please, share it with me so we can find a solution for it."

"I can't."

"Listen, Darling, together we can lick anything. If you'd let me help you, we could get back on an even keel. But as long as you shut me out, I'm helpless."

"It's nothing." Phyllis raised her head and made a ghastly attempt at a smile. "I'm just being feminine and silly. Come on, you get Lindsay and we'll have breakfast."

In early November framing started on the dream house. The sub-floor was laid and the skeleton of all of the outer walls and most of the inner walls were up when Keith sat at his

175

drafting table in the dark one night, staring out the window. He wasn't seeing the yard below him, the last of the golden football mums making a faint lightness in the perennial border. The leaves were gone from the ornamental trees but the crabapples still retained some of their small red globes. There was a slight wind that set the boughs dipping and swaying. But Keith was seeing with his mind's eye, not his physical eyes, and what he saw put a little smile on his face.

The picture in his mind was of his family in the dream house. He would be in his workroom in the studio, across the lawn, Phyllis would be busy in the kitchen or perhaps relaxing in the living room. Between them, on the lawn, Lindsay would be playing with Pepper. It was an idyllic picture and he was fiercely concentrated on it because he didn't want to think about the reality of his life, particularly the shambles that his marriage had become.

Phyllis walked briskly into the room, flipped on the lights and closed the door. She was dressed in her red woolen coat, carrying her purse and a pair of gloves. She was beautiful, chic, and a stranger to him. He stood and looked at her, speechless with foreboding.

When she spoke, her voice was hard and impersonal. "I'm sorry to be blunt but I don't know how else to say it. I've been having an affair with Roger Otis and I'm going away with him now."

Keith just looked at her, stunned and disbelieving.

"Don't look at me like that," Phyllis said, irritated.

"You're going away with Roger?"

"Yes."

"I see." Keith's mind raced, putting together the hints and fragments of knowledge that he had forbidden his mind to deal with. Suddenly an awful thought struck him. "You're not taking Lindsay," he declared.

"No. She'll be better off here with you. She prefers you anyway." She cast a fleeting glance at the small easel next to Keith's drafting table and the little desk and chair. There was a painting on the easel, swirls of blue and pink, purple and gold. Her heart seemed to contract in a painful spasm but she sternly quelled it, refusing to acknowledge the hurt.

"Phyllis, why?"

"I don't love you anymore. I fell in love with Roger and he loves me, too."

"When did all this happen?"

"It started when you took that trip to Santa Cruz without me last spring."

"I wanted you to come with me."

Phyllis made a gesture of dismissal. "What's

the use? I don't want to go over and over it. You had your little fling with Merrilee -- you needn't think I didn't see through your pretence that it was all for Kurt. I saw you together at Vi's party, you were certainly not brotherly with her that night. And you've had all those "business trips" with Alicia. I'm supposed to believe they were strictly business, purely platonic? Please. So don't go all holy on me now."

"There was never anything between Merrilee and me. And Alicia's my partner. She and Del are happily married. I thought I was happily married."

"Nothing lasts forever, Keith."

"What can I say to Lindsay?"

"Tell her I died. She'll soon forget all about me."

Phyllis turned and went out, closing the door behind her. He heard her high heels clicking on the hardwood floor of the hall and down the stairs.

CHAPTER 13

Keith eventually went to bed but he didn't sleep that night. The next morning he called his mother and explained what had happened. He asked her if he could leave Lindsay with her for the morning. Dextra was horrified but not really surprised at her daughter-in-law's defection. She had been expecting some kind of blowup for quite awhile. She agreed to stop by and pick Lindsay up on her way to work.

Lindsay loved to visit Grandma and Grandpa in their store; it was filled with fascinating things and they had given her a drawer of her own in the big desk in the back room where she could keep the treasures they gave her -- erasers in dozens of shapes and sizes, all kinds and colors of paper, crayons, colored pencils, even a real book with blank pages to write her own stories in. It had butterflies on the cover.

Lindsay thought life couldn't ever be any better than to have a real book of her very own with butterflies on the cover. Sometimes she read

179

Grandma or Grandpa or Daddy what she "wrote" in her book; she was a little puzzled why they couldn't read it for themselves. They could read so many other things. In the end she filed it away as just one more example of the illogic and arbitrariness of grownups.

Keith was downstairs at the kitchen table drinking coffee when Lindsay and Pepper came downstairs. He let Pepper out into the back yard then sat down and picked Lindsay up. She had her painting from the easel in one hand and her penguin under the other arm. She handed him the painting.

"It's finished," she said.

"I like it very much," Keith said honestly. "Especially that patch of color."

"There's too much blue in it," Lindsay said critically. "I like it better where there's more purple."

"Purple's good," Keith agreed.

He stood up and sat her in her chair and proceeded to get breakfast for them. Crisp bacon from the microwave and scrambled eggs from the stove top. Lindsay asserted her right to help by making the toast. He smiled at her as she very seriously undertook the task. She pushed her chair over to the counter, got the bread out of the refrigerator and climbed up on the chair. She opened the bread and the toaster-oven and watched intently as the bread browned to the exact shade she desired. She pressed the lever and carefully pulled the toast out onto a plate.

"Where's Mommy?" Lindsay asked, as they ate.

"She had to go somewhere. You know what? Grandma's going to stop and pick you up so you can spend the morning at the store. How about that?"

"That's pretty fine. I better get dressed."

She picked up the piece of bacon on her plate and slipped to the floor. Keith watched her scamper upstairs, his heart bursting with love and loss. He let Pepper in, fed her, and then cleaned up the dishes.

After Dextra picked Lindsay up, Keith barely gave his secretary/receptionist time to get to the office and get a cup of coffee before he called. When Stan transferred him to Alicia, he told her briefly that Phyllis was gone and then cut in on her exclamations of dismay and sympathy.

"Listen, do me a favor, will you? Go out to my house site and call the contractor off. I want the work stopped today."

Alicia wanted to come right over and talk to him. He didn't want to talk to anyone but he saw the inevitability of it.

"Sure, come ahead. But first talk to the contractor, will you?"

After the first couple of weeks, the strangeness of being a single parent began to wear off and he and Lindsay established a routine. Keith was quite happy taking care of Lindsay morning and evening and weekends but he couldn't travel with her and he didn't think it would be right for her to spend her days at the office with him. He asked his mother for advice in finding a housekeeper who would live in and take care of Lindsay. After some searching, interviewing, and heartburnings, his mother presented him with Alma Gregg. She was widowed, in her early forties, and her own children were grown and out of the nest. She was not trained to do anything commercial and her natural bent was to motherhood and homemaking. Keith was enchanted and hired her almost the moment he looked into her calm, dark eyes and saw that the lines in her face were set into patterns denoting a cheerful disposition.

Alma hadn't been in the house a week before Keith knew that she was a jewel beyond price. Lindsay took to her right away and Alma fell in love with the little girl on sight. But she was no patsy -- Alma knew when to be firm and how to be firm. Lindsay soon learned that there were limits and, although she pushed, she respected Alma's rules.

The house was a large one so when he had a

bedroom redecorated for Alma, Keith redecorated one of the other bedrooms for himself. The room he'd shared with Phyllis held too many memories, too many emotions to be comfortable. He chose a large room that overlooked the driveway from one window and the back yard from the other. Since there was no one to please but himself, he used the colors and patterns he liked and was very well pleased with his green and white bower. Lindsay was excited about Daddy's new bedroom and gravely helped him choose sheets and a bedspread when it was finished.

A few weeks after Alma's advent, Lindsay celebrated her fourth birthday. She had a party in the afternoon, with a dozen or so children from around the neighborhood with whom she played. Grandma and Grandpa stopped by on their way home from work and gave her their gifts, a real china tea set with pink roses on it from Grandma and a scooter from Grandpa with wheels that had blue lights that lit up when you rode it. And, of course, a pretty little frilly dress of pink with white socks with pink lace around the tops and various bows and barrettes, also mostly pink. Lindsay thanked Dextra politely but privately wished the dress was royal blue and that the socks didn't have lace on them.

Lindsay and Grandpa and Pepper were out on

the sidewalk playing with the scooter, while Grandma sat on the front porch and watched, when Keith drove into the driveway. Lindsay ran to him, chattering happily of her party and her presents and her scooter. He bent down to pet Pepper, sending the dog into transports of delight, then picked Lindsay up and perched her on his shoulder. He greeted his parents and they all sat on the front porch in the gathering dusk while Lindsay showed him her presents and demonstrated the wonderfulness of the scooter.

Then they all went out to dinner, including Alma. Keith reflected often that he was extremely fortunate to have such a caring woman looking after Lindsay and made it a point to treat her as family and not as hired help. Alma repaid his thoughtfulness with her devotion to Lindsay and her unfailing good humor. In deference to Lindsay's tastes, since it was her birthday dinner, they went to a little cafe halfway between Talent and Ashland where fried chicken was the specialty of the house. They had a hilarious time but Keith noticed that Lindsay seemed to flag about halfway through the meal. He ascribed it to tiredness after the excitement of the day.

That night, after her bath, Lindsay came downstairs in her jammies and robe, holding her penguin but without a book, Pepper by her side. Keith set his own book down and took her up on his lap. Pepper sat on her haunches and looked at them expectantly.

"What no book tonight? Where's *Hiawatha*? And Tail-Up-Straight and Short-Hair?"

Lindsay looked deeply into his eyes and Keith stirred uneasily. She had never looked at him just like that before and he knew that whatever she had to say was very important to her.

"Where's my mommy?" she asked solemnly.

"Lindy, your mommy's dead." As soon as he said it, he regretted the lie, but he didn't know how to retract it.

"Dead? But you said she went away."

"I didn't think you were old enough to understand. That was when you were only three. But now you're four years old and you can understand lots of things you couldn't before."

Lindsay nodded thoughtfully. "Did Mommy go to Heaven?"

"I expect she did," he said.

"Won't she ever come home?"

Pepper didn't understand this change in the routine of her people but she knew that something was not right. She put one paw on Keith's knee and whined. He petted her head absently.

"No, Sweetheart. Your mommy won't ever come home."

"How did she get dead, Daddy?"

"She got sick and the doctor couldn't make her well."

"Like Sue Pohl's dog? He got sick and the doctor put him to sleep. Did the doctor put Mommy to sleep?"

"No, the doctor tried to help your mommy but she was too sick." That, at least, Keith reflected fleetingly, was true, all but the part about the doctor.

"I miss Mommy. Don't you?"

"Yes, I do."

"Sue Pohl was real sad about her dog. Are you sad about Mommy?"

"Very sad. But you and I still have each other."

"I love you, Daddy."

Lindsay put her arms around his neck and held on tightly. He held her close, careful not to squeeze too hard. She relaxed her hold but remained snuggled close to him. He looked down to see tears sliding out from under her closed eyelids.

"Can I have a picture of Mommy?" Lindsay asked.

"Of course. Shall we get it now?"

Lindsay nodded and he carried her up to the workroom, Pepper trailing worriedly behind. There were a lot of snapshots and photos in a couple of drawers and a box full of them in the closet. Keith set them on his desk and, with Lindsay on his lap, they went through them. At the bottom of one of the drawers, there was a manila envelope of wedding pictures. Keith was suddenly filled with pain and longing but he set his feelings aside so he could tend to Lindsay. She looked at each photograph carefully, then looked up at her father.

"Can I have two pictures, Daddy?"

"Certainly."

Lindsay selected a head shot of Phyllis, taken three-quarter face with her bridal headdress in place and a soft, sweet smile on her lips and in her eyes. Then she choose one of Keith and Phyllis dancing the first dance at the reception. The two of them were gazing into each other's eyes as if they were the only two people in the world and the crowd around them mere cardboard cut-outs.

"Okay," Keith began and had to stop and clear his throat. "Okay, Short Stuff, tomorrow we'll go shopping and get you a couple of picture frames."

The next day they made a foray into the shops and boutiques that permeated the Shakespeare theater district. The tourist crowd was gone until the festival the next summer and many of the shops had a sort of "lying fallow" feeling about them. But Lindsay was thrilled and chattered excitedly as they wandered in and out of the myriad specialty stores. She wasn't interested in the ersatz Tudor souvenirs with their fake coats of arms but she loved the bookstores and the shops with candles and incense. Keith delighted her with a pair of hand-dipped bayberry candles and a pair of china swans to hold them, along with a crystal unicorn ring stand for Alma. When they found a shop that sold picture frames, Lindsay surveyed the selection as gravely as she did most things and pronounced the majority of them either silly or ugly.

"I don't like any of these," she stated with finality.

Keith was dismayed. He had enjoyed their shopping trip thus far but he did have an appointment early in the afternoon and he had planned to take his daughter to lunch as long as they were downtown.

"None of them? But, Sweetheart, surely you can find one or two that you like." He held a lovely crystal frame with a rose sculpted on a lower corner so she could see it better. "This is a beautiful frame. Don't you think so? See, it even has a rose carved on it."

"I like the frame and I like the rose," Lindsay agreed. "But I want a picture of Mommy, not that lady."

Involuntarily, Keith laughed. Seeing the hurt in Lindsay's face, he stifled his mirth. "I'm sorry, Lindsay, I didn't mean to hurt your feelings. See, the lady's picture comes out so we can put any picture we want to in the frame." He opened the back of the frame and took a smugly perky model's photo out. "There, see?"

Lindsay nodded, smiling happily. "We can put Mommy in when we get home."

Life was good for Keith once he got over Phyllis' defection and the consequent divorce. She had opted to go to Reno for the divorce and asked for no settlement, no alimony, and no visitation rights. Then she had disappeared. For a couple of years he would hear a bit about her from people who knew Marcia Otis then he heard that Phyllis and Roger had split up and he heard no more about her. His business continued to prosper and he enjoyed his work. He also enjoyed his social life. As a very presentable and eligible bachelor, he was popular with hostesses who needed a man to balance a dinner table when the guests were all couples except for one single lady.

The way Phyllis left him and the reason she gave sent him back to a modification of his original, adolescent perception of women; they were good for sex but a nuisance around the home unless in the capacity of paid employee. He dated a lot but was very careful not to let any woman get close enough for him to have an emotional attachment to her. He carefully concealed his emotional wounds and enjoyed the company of a number of attractive young women. The moment any woman gave any intimation of love for him, he dropped her, moving on to the next without ever looking back.

It was Lindsay who gave meaning and joyousness to his life. He made sure she had the means for creative expression and intellectual development as well as everything necessary for her physical development. As a rule she was very good -- obedient and desirous of pleasing him and Alma. She could also be exceedingly naughty on occasion. One summer afternoon when she was five, Keith came in the back door to the kitchen, following the garden hose to find out why on earth it was in the house. He found his darling daughter wearing a yellow rain slicker, snow boots, and a black baseball cap with the bill turned backwards. She was standing on the counter spraying the room. Beside her on a trivet was a freshly-baked peach pie. Fortunately, the nozzle of the hose was set to a fine spray and not a high-pressure stream.

Lindsay heard Keith come into the room and turned toward him, the nozzle of the hose turning with her so that he was liberally soaked before he had much more than bellowed her name.

"Lindsay! What the hell are you doing?"

She smiled at him. "Hi, Daddy. I'm a fireman. I have to squirt out the fire."

"Well, I'm not on fire!"

Keith took the nozzle from her and turned it off. He was furious with his small daughter, who he knew was perfectly well aware of the naughtiness of hosing down the kitchen. At that moment he could have spanked her with great satisfaction. By the time he had tossed the hose out the back door he had seen the humor in her joke. He lifted Lindsay down off the counter, fighting back an urge to laugh.

"Who's going to clean all this up?" he demanded as sternly as he could, knowing that Lindsay was an expert at detecting the twinkle in his eye, however hard he tried to hide it.

"Alma."

"I don't think so."

"Daddy will," Lindsay said, giving him her most charming smile.

"I don't think so."

Lindsay turned her palms up and shrugged. "I don't know who."

"I do. Lindsay's going to clean it up."

Lindsay shook her head regretfully. "Lindsay's too little."

Keith shook his head back at her. He fetched the mop and bucket and set her to work mopping up the water on the floor while he got a couple of kitchen towels and started to mop up the water on the counters and cupboards. Alma came in from the living room, carrying a dust cloth and spray bottle of furniture polish. She stopped short and stared at the mess.

"What happened to this kitchen? And my pie! Look at it," she exclaimed.

Keith looked at Lindsay who was too busy mopping to look up.

"Lindsay. Alma wants to know what happened to her kitchen," Keith said severely.

Lindsay put the mop in the bucket and went to put her hand in Alma's, looking up at her with a bright smile.

"I like you, Alma," Lindsay said.

"I like you, too, Lindsay," Alma replied, beginning to get the hang of the situation.

"Never mind that, now," Keith said. "Explain to Alma what happened to her kitchen."

"A fireman came and squirted out the fire. Isn't it lucky the house isn't burned down?"

Alma shot a startled look at Keith. He shook his head.

"Yes, I'm very glad the house isn't burned down. What kind of fire was it?" Alma asked.

"It was 'maginary," Lindsay explained

earnestly. "But it was a bad one. The flames were shooting up all over and your pie was on fire and everything."

"And who was this fireman who put out the imaginary fire?" asked Alma.

"Me!" Lindsay announced triumphantly. "I put out every bit of the fire all by myself."

"I see." Alma was having the same trouble Keith was in keeping a straight face. She knew well enough that Lindsay thought she was getting away with something but she was so funny about it that neither of them had the heart to scold her. "I don't think we'd better have any more imaginary fires. I don't like to find my kitchen in such a mess. And the pie I worked hard to bake this morning is ruined and that is a waste of my time and work and your dad's money that bought the ingredients."

"I don't think there'll be any more fires," Lindsay said comfortingly. "And me and Daddy are cleaning up all the water, aren't we, Dad?"

"That we are. So get back to work."

Alma protested. "You go on with what you were doing, Keith. Lindsay and I'll get this."

"That's okay," he said. "I want her to see just how much extra work and inconvenience she's caused."

"Those firemen sure were messy, huh?" Lindsay said wonderingly.

CHAPTER 14

The Kovaceks and the Janowskis didn't see much of each other for several years. They were all busy, the Janowskis with their ranch and their extended family, the Kovaceks with architecture and Lindsay. So Keith was surprised one afternoon early in Lindsay's fifteenth spring to find Jazzy on his doorstep when he answered the bell. Jazzy had become a little top-heavy with the years and Lora's good cooking but he was still a handsome man. He wore jeans and a western shirt with cowboy boots and hat; his hair hung in long braids and was still black with just a few strands of silver. Keith had retained his boyish figure through strictly foregoing certain foods and with regular workouts at the club. He dressed in slacks and open-necked shirts with cowboy boots; he rarely wore a hat of any kind. On the whole, the years had been kind to both men.

"Jazzy!" Keith exclaimed delightedly.

They shook hands but it wasn't enough, they

threw their arms around one another, pounding each other's back.

"It's been too long, Keith," Jazzy said.

"It has, son, it has. Come on in. Where's Lora, didn't she come with you?"

Keith led the way into the living room and waved Jazzy to a chair.

"No, she didn't come this trip. One of her nieces had a baby a few days ago and she's over there helping out."

"That sounds like Lora, sure enough. How've you been?"

"We're fine." Jazzy amended his statement. "Well, no rancher's fine these days, not in this country. But we're okay."

"Market's still shot to hell, I know."

"Yeah. The damn politicians keep screwing with the prices, trying to guarantee cheap food for city people. Don't get me started. Anyway, this last go-round has about flattened me. But I got to talking to Charley Elmore -- you remember Charley."

"Sure. It was him locked the home ec teacher -- what was her name? Ms. Schneider! That's right, Ms. Schneider -- in his locker that time."

They laughed, then Keith looked around guiltily for Lindsay.

"Got himself suspended, too," Jazzy said with a grin.

"I never could figure out why the board thought suspension was such a terrible punishment. Charley never wanted anything better than to be suspended. Hey, you want a beer?"

"Yeah, I do. Talking's dry work and I'm going to talk a lot."

Keith went out to the kitchen and Jazzy followed him. Keith took two longnecks out of the refrigerator and twisted the caps off. He mimed pouring and Jazzy shook his head, as Keith had known he would. They took their beers out the back door and settled down in the shade in a couple of padded redwood lawn chairs. The perennial border was a mass of blossoms -- iris with their orchid-like petals, glowing pink and blue and yellow and white; lupines in their clumps of tall pastel columns of blooms; violets creeping out into the lawn with their dainty heart-shaped leaves and delicate purple flowers. The trees and shrubs made living walls on three sides of the yard, frothy with scented bloom -- panicles of old-fashioned lilacs, viburnum heavy with snowballs, arching branches of pink bleeding hearts, the miniature pink bouquets of the hawthorns. It was so beautiful it nearly took Jazzy's breath away.

"Nice," Jazzy approved. "It's real nice out here."

"Yeah, thanks."

They went through the "how are your folks, fine, how are yours" routine, each glad that there was no bad news either to give or receive. Then Jazzy got down to business.

"What do you know about dude ranches?" he asked.

"I know there are such things. That's about it."

"Charley and his wife -- he married one of those rich Porter girls from over near Olene six or seven years ago -- went to a dude ranch out of Wickenburg and Charley was telling me about it. I can hardly feature Charley at a dude ranch, though."

Keith laughed. "Neither can I. How is old Charley? Same as ever?"

"About the same. Him and his brother Jess are farming their home place. They planted twenty acres of carrots this spring."

"Carrots?" Keith was surprised. He'd never heard of anyone growing carrots over in the Klamath Basin. "They growing okay?"

Jazzy grinned. "They're growing fine as frog hair. The problem's going to be getting them out of the ground come fall."

"Spud equipment work on them?"

Jazzy laughed. "Charley and Jess sure do hope so."

Keith laughed with him. "I bet they do."

"Anyways, Charley was telling me about this dude ranch. Charge a mint of money and people come from all over the country. From out of the country, too. Charley said there were some Germans there getting a hell of a kick out of being in the American wild west. The cowboys routed everyone out about dawn for trail riding, even packing in trips."

"Sounds like it could be fun with the right bunch."

"I'm glad you think so," Jazzy said. "Because Lora and I've been thinking we could turn our place into a dude ranch. Keep a few head of cattle to amaze the city-slickers and a few to butcher and feed 'em."

"Might be a shrewd move, Jazzy."

"We think so. What we need is some idea how much it would cost to change over and exactly what we'd have to build to get started."

"Yeah, I see what you mean. I could do some research, see what the general layout is. That what you want?"

Jazzy nodded. "See, Lora and I went and stayed at that one Charley was telling us about. And we liked the setup. We can do that. We took a mess of pictures. Here, I brought them with me."

Keith took the pictures from him and flipped

through them rapidly.

"Let's take them up to my workroom," he suggested. "We can spread them out there."

He snagged them each another beer as they went through the kitchen. They found Lindsay in the workroom, seated at the computer, busily writing a term paper.

"Lindsay, come give your old Uncle Jazzy a hug."

Lindsay looked over her shoulder and bounced up, beaming at him. She hurled herself across the room and into his arms.

"Jazzy! It's about time you came to see us. Where's Lora?"

"Someone had to stay and tend to business." He grinned at her, holding her at arm's length and looking her over carefully. "Keith, the girl's a knockout."

Lindsay was a pretty girl, in spite of her ugly, fashionable clothes. She wore light blue denim overalls that had been ripped here and there and had uneven bleached streaks. An oversized camo t-shirt added an effect of dreariness. She finished the ensemble with a pair of unlaced clumping work boots, artistically scraped and scarred. Her hair looked as if she had bunched it at random into little tufts, using clips of various shapes and sizes, although Jazzy was sure she had taken great pains to get exactly the effect she wanted.

Lindsay was slightly built like her mother but her facial features were Keith's, cast in a feminine mold. She was not actually a knockout but it was clear that in another two or three years she would be, in spite of her campaign of uglification in the name of fashion.

Keith looked at his daughter with trepidation. "Yeah, I know."

"Well, don't take it so hard, son," Jazzy said, laughing.

Lindsay laughed with Jazzy then went to the computer, pushed the save button, and closed her file.

"It's easy for you to talk. You don't have to keep guys like Pat Seakert away from her."

"Chickens coming home to roost?" Jazzy inquired.

"I don't know what you mean," Keith declared.

He cleared his slope and began to lay Jazzy's photos out in rows.

"Have a seat," he invited, nodding at a high stool.

Jazzy sat down, hooking his boot heels over a rung. Lindsay swiveled around to face the men.

"Tell me about Daddy when he was my age. I bet he was wilder than a turpentined cat."

Keith scowled at her. "I don't know where you pick up those revolting expressions. Don't you have homework?"

Jazzy laughed. "I love it. Keith Kovacek playing the heavy father."

Lindsay winked at Jazzy and answered her father. "Yes, sir. I told Sue I'd come over and we could do our geometry together." She picked up her geometry book and a spiral notebook. As she went past him on her way out, she spoke conspiratorially to Jazzy, "You can tell me sometime when he's not around."

"Study hard, now, you hear?" Jazzy admonished her as she went out the door.

"And be back in time for dinner," Keith called.

Lindsay laughed as she went down the hall. "Fuss, fuss, fuss."

The front door opened and closed. Keith looked at Jazzy and shook his head helplessly.

Jazzy smiled reassuringly. "She's a good kid, Keith."

"I know. It's just that you worry, you know?"

Jazzy nodded. "I know you're a pretty successful architect."

"Middling. Yes, I guess I am."

"I expect that means expensive. That's okay, no reason why you shouldn't charge what you're worth. Thing is, we don't have a lot of capital."

Keith started to speak but Jazzy rushed on.

"We can get some backing from the bank and

the cattle will bring in some money. What I'm getting at, would you maybe take a percentage of the ranch instead of a cash fee?"

"You know I'd be glad to do it for the fun of it. No charge. Not to you and Lora."

"That wouldn't be right. We couldn't let you do that."

Keith could see by the stubborn set of Jazzy's jaw that there was no way he was going to win that argument.

"All right," he said with a smile, "you can buy me out later. After it's a going concern."

"Well, we can leave it like that for now. I expect we'd better hatch some chickens before we go to counting them."

They spent the rest of the afternoon studying the photos, exchanging ideas, discussing possibilities and just plain enjoying one another's company. Finally, Jazzy stood up and held out his hand. Keith rose and they shook.

"Could you and Lora put up with Lindsay and me for a few days sometime soon? I'll need to scope out the site."

"Anytime. I appreciate this, Keith."

"Don't thank me. I have an idea it's going to be one of the best investments I've ever made."

Keith and Lindsay spent the next weekend at the Janowski ranch. Lindsay had a great time horseback riding and pitching in with the barn chores with an assortment of Jazzy and Lora's nieces, nephews, and cousins of various degrees. Keith and Jazzy spent most of the time walking around, discussing what new buildings would be necessary and which existing buildings would have to be modified or replaced. They roped Lora into their talks when they could but she was content to let the two of them do the planning.

Jazzy wanted to get the project underway as quickly as possible so Keith worked hard designing and drawing up blueprints. He even got his partner, Alicia Mathison, interested in the project to the point where she worked on the plans. Keith went out to the ranch as often as he could to supervise the work and make sure Jazzy and Lora were happy with it. Alicia and Lindsay accompanied him one Saturday. Workmen were surveying for the cabin foundations and another crew was unloading building materials.

Keith had an idea for a swimming pool that would minimize the cost of building and maintaining it while keeping it congruent with the setting. He led Jazzy, Lora, and Alicia across the meadow to the creek. The setting itself was spectacular. The ranch house, barn, and outbuildings stood toward the bottom of a wooded slope with a wide meadow below. At the bottom of the meadow, just before the forest started up the hill, ran a creek. The banks of the creek were lined with quaking aspens; here and there stood ancient cottonwoods.

"We'll widen the creek and build a dam," Keith said, pointing to a spot well downstream from a shallow rapids. "We can scoop out a hole to make it deeper, at least at the dam end. But we'll let the rapids alone. They'll be fun to wade in and they're very picturesque. Alicia, did Stan get that report on the water rights?"

"Yes, it's in my briefcase. No problem."

"And the environmental impact stuff?"

"We're still filing papers but it looks like everything's okay. I'll stay on it until we get a definite go-ahead."

Lindsay came dashing up to them on the back of a pretty chestnut mare, just a little too fast and just a little too close for courtesy. She sat and grinned at them. The mare fidgeted, tossing her head and chewing the bit. Lora stepped over and reset the bit, stroking the mare's muzzle and murmuring gently to her. Keith frowned at Lindsay then turned back to the grownups.

"We can line the dam and the pool with rocks to minimize the damage to the creek and keep the banks from washing away," he explained.

"That'll make the Sierra Club happy, I hope," Jazzy said. "Although, maybe it won't. It's kind of hard to tell sometimes what will and what won't."

"I think it'll be much better than a concrete pool." Lora glanced back at the house. "I could hardly reconcile myself to a regular pool. It would just be too incongruous out here."

Alicia nodded. "And this way the pool will be self cleaning and there'll be no need for chemicals or a lot of expensive pumps and equipment. This is going to be a completely organic complex."

"Organic?" Lindsay interjected. "I thought organic mean shit."

"Lindsay!" Keith was becoming quite irritated with his daughter. Girls of fifteen were, he seemed to remember, alternately bratty and sweet. Little girls one minute, sophisticated ladies the next. It had confused him when he was fifteen and it confused him now. He hoped he would be able to cope but he was by no means certain that he could.

"Sorry, Pop. I mean manure."

She reined the mare around and cued her to gallop.

CHAPTER 15

The house next door to the Kovaceks had been vacant for a couple of months when Keith and Lindsay pulled into their driveway early one summer evening to find a young man in the front yard and every evidence of new residents. Keith had been on a business trip to Boise and Lindsay had picked him up at the Medford airport. Keith was driving and the car was a silver blue Mercedes convertible that Lindsay was normally forbidden to touch. Her car, a little green second-hand Plymouth was parked in the garage. Keith parked and walked over to the fence. Lindsay followed him.

The young man was tall and straight with wide shoulders; he moved like an athlete as he picked up a child-size girl's bike from the front walk and wheeled it toward the garage. He and Lindsay were frankly appraising one another. Both seemed to approve of what they saw. Keith took one look at the gold ring dangling from the guy's pierced eyebrow and snorted inwardly. He was too polite to show his disapproval openly -- after all it was none of his business if the kid wanted to pierce every pierceable spot on his body. The oversized t-shirt cropped just above the waist with the Tasmanian Devil emblazoned across the chest and the jeans so baggy that a couple of inches of his underwear showed didn't help. Then Keith reflected that he was being a little harsh in his reaction to this boy, considering that Lindsay was wearing a blue denim mini skirt with an indigo rhinestone studded t-shirt.

"Hi," Keith said.

The boy wheeled the bike over to the fence and smiled shyly at Lindsay. "Hi."

Lindsay held her hand out and he shook with her.

"You're our new neighbor?" she asked, with a welcoming smile.

"Yeah. Scott Markham."

"I'm Lindsay Kovacek. This is my dad, Keith."

Keith and Scott shook hands.

"Nice to meet you, Scott," Keith said. "Where did you move from?"

"Eugene."

"What do you think? You going to like it here in this quiet little town after living in Eugene?"

Scott glanced at Lindsay then said, "Yes, sir,

I think so."

Lindsay smiled at him. Keith frowned. "Come on, Lindsay, we'd better get the bags inside and see about dinner. See you, Scott."

Keith went over to the car. Lindsay and Scott exchanged smiles and she went to help Keith. She unlocked the front door and held it open for him. He set his bags down in the foyer. Lindsay closed the door and took some envelopes out of the wire basket under the mail slot. She dropped her purse onto a chair and flipped through the mail, took out a couple of envelopes then handed the rest to Keith. They went into the living room and sat down to open their letters. After a few minutes, Lindsay tossed hers onto an end table.

"What does Alma say?" she asked. "When is she coming home?"

"Maybe next week. Her daughter is still in the hospital and they haven't found out what's wrong yet."

The phone rang and Lindsay jumped up to answer it. Keith went out to the kitchen and brought back a beer for himself and a cola for Lindsay. She replaced the handset on the base.

"Thanks," she said, taking the soda from him. "That was Sue. We're going to a movie. And I'm going to stay at her house tonight. Okay?"

"What are you going to see?"

"Don't hype out, Pop. It's only "R" rated. Can

I take the Mercedes?"

"Nope, if you're going out, I'm going to need it myself. What's wrong with your car?"

"Like, it's not a Mercedes."

Keith grinned at her. "Like, too bad."

Lindsay kissed him and picked up her purse. "It never hurts to try."

"Behave yourself."

"Yeah, you, too." She laughed and went out the door.

Keith called one of the women with whom he was on intimate terms and invited her to dinner. Sunny Grantham was a glamour girl of around thirty, blond, blue-eyed, with a spectacular figure of which she was very proud. Keith considered her dumber than dirt but she possessed talents that made conversation a waste of time. For intellectual stimulation he could always tune in the History Channel or go to the library.

He showered and changed into slacks and an open-necked shirt. He didn't bother to turn on the light as he started downstairs so when he glanced out the window at the head of the stairs he could see into the house next door. Through a lighted, undraped upstairs window he could see a woman dancing. Evidently she was standing on some kind of mini trampoline because she bounced as well as jiggled. Keith stopped for a moment to look. He couldn't see her face but from the way she moved, he guessed her to be old enough to be Scott's mother. Probably she was Scott's mother. She was dressed in black slacks with a loose red top. Her body was unfashionably plump and her dark hair was shoulder-length, flying every which way as she gyrated to a very quick rhythm. He enjoyed watching her for a minute or two then forgot all about her as he got into the Mercedes and backed out of the driveway.

Keith thoroughly approved of Sunny's appearance when he picked her up. She was wearing a sundress of some silky fabric, with pink and purple flowers on a white background. The bodice was low-cut and the full skirt was high-cut. High-heeled sandals with a matching purple clutch purse completed her ensemble. He took her to an expensive restaurant where they had a couple of drinks before dinner and a liqueur after. They had been dating for several months and Sunny harbored the hope that he would propose if she was sufficiently sexy, thus she had never made any objection to winding up their dates in a motel room. That night, with Lindsay at Sue Pohl's for the night and Alma in Baton Rouge with her daughter, he took Sunny home with him.

The moon had not yet risen and the street light was too far away to illuminate his front yard or driveway but the starlight was enough to make out the location of the front walk and porch steps. Keith parked the car and set the hand brake. He and Sunny indulged in a little foreplay before he went around and opened the car door for her. She stepped out and they went up the walk arm-in-arm. As they went up the steps, something hurtled from the porch and struck Keith squarely on the hip bone. He fell backwards, being unable to regain his balance due to his arm and Sunny's being intertwined. As he fell, he dragged Sunny with him and she fell partly on him and partly on the sidewalk. She screamed and something on the porch set up a shrieking fit to wake the dead.

"What the hell!" Keith yelled.

He got to his feet and pulled Sunny to hers. Suddenly a flashlight shone and the light fastened on his face, effectively blinding him. He put up a hand to ward it off.

"What the hell are you doing?" He demanded. "Take that light out of my face, damn you! Who are you, anyway? And what are you doing on my front porch?"

The light left Keith's face, flitted across Sunny's and then fell to the sidewalk.

"Why don't you look where you're going?" a sassy child's voice countered.

Keith could see part of a boy child in the

flashlight and he could see that a girl child joined him.

"Give me that light for a minute," he said.

He took it out of the boy's hand and briefly shone it over the two children. Geoffrey and Allison Markham were nine and eight, respectively. Both had short curly blond hair and, although Keith couldn't see the color of their eyes in that light, he supposed (correctly) that they were blue. They were cuter than a basketful of puppies, even when they looked half-defiant, half-scared. He handed the flashlight back to Geoffrey.

"It's not a burglar, it's just the guy that lives here, Geoffrey," Allison declared.

"Where do you belong?" Keith asked more gently.

"We're detectives. We saw some suspicious movements in front of your house and we came to investigate," Geoffrey explained.

"I told him it was a dog. But he said that was no fun. So we came to make sure because it might be a burglar or a cereal killer," Allison chimed in.

"Yeah, the neighborhood's crawling with them. Let's go."

"Where? We haven't finished investigating yet," Geoffrey objected.

"You've investigated all you're going to

tonight. Come on, I'm taking you home."

"You don't have to take us," Geoffrey protested. "We live right over there."

"Yes, but I want to make sure your mother keeps you in. I'll be right back, Sunny." Keith handed her his key ring. "Go on in and make yourself at home."

Sunny was very angry but she took the keys and went up the steps. Keith shepherded the children across the driveway and around to the back porch of their own house. He rapped on the door but Geoffrey opened it and the two kids scuttled inside to stand behind their mother, who was astonished to find her children and a strange man on her doorstep at nearly midnight. She looked bewilderedly from them to Keith and back to them.

"Allison? Geoffrey? What on earth?"

Keith found that he was not nearly as irritated as he'd thought he was. Mrs. Markham was not glamorous nor was she a beauty. She was pleasant to look upon and Keith had the impression that she was a woman of character, that she would be dependable, a comfortable companion. He found his voice, prodded by her inquiring look.

"I'm Keith Kovacek, your neighbor across the way. I fell over these two on my front steps just now. I thought you might like to know where they are."

"On your front steps?" She turned to the children, "Upstairs. Go to bed. We'll have this out in the morning."

"Come on, Mom," Geoffrey started.

"Do we have to?" Allison demanded.

"Yes. You have to. Not another word. Go on."

Rather to Keith's surprise, they went. He called good nights after them but they ignored him. Mrs. Markham turned back to him.

"I'm sorry they bothered you, Mr. Kovacek."

Keith saw that she was looking at his hand with great concern. He looked and saw that he had acquired a bloody scrape.

"Come on in, let me put something on that."

Keith allowed her to lead him over to the kitchen sink and he obediently stuck his hand under the faucet when she turned the water on and gestured for him to do so.

"I didn't realize that you meant you literally fell over my kids," she said.

She pulled a first aid kit from an otherwise empty drawer and set it on the breakfast bar. She pulled a couple of paper towels from the roll and turned off the water. She patted his hand dry and to his own surprise he allowed her to direct him to sit on a stool while she rendered first aid.

"I always unpack the first aid kit first thing,"

she told him with a smile. "It seems the kids are constantly getting cut or scraped or stung or something."

She sprayed the scrape with antiseptic and applied a G.I. Joe bandage. He looked askance at that and she grinned at him.

"I know. But just think, it could have been a Barbie Doll bandage. You should be glad it was Geoffrey's turn to choose."

"Oh, I am, I am. I really don't think I could cope with a Barbie Doll bandage on my hand."

She laughed. "I don't have any lollipops but would you like a drink for being such a good, brave boy? Scotch, vodka, Jack Daniels, or coffee?"

"Scotch and water, please."

While she made his drink and one for herself, he looked around. The room was chaotic with boxes, packed, half-packed, and empty. Stacks of dishes and kitchenware covered most surfaces and he found himself approving her taste in color and form.

She set a glass down in front of him and took hers around to the other side of the bar and sat down.

"Thanks," Keith said. "Welcome to Ashland."

"Now how do you know I'm new in town?"

"My daughter and I met Scott this afternoon. He said you'd moved from Eugene."

Mrs. Markham nodded. "As a matter of fact, Scott took the train back to Eugene a couple of hours ago, to visit his father. We're divorced. I've seen your daughter coming and going. She's very pretty."

"Yeah, she is, although I don't know how you can tell through all the makeup and hideous clothes."

"Oh, well, I guess every generation that comes up has to have some way to shock their parents. I remember the first time my parents saw me light a cigarette. They nearly passed out. You'd have thought I'd broken all ten commandments and violated most of the criminal statutes in one fell swoop."

Keith laughed and she joined in. He drained his glass and stood up.

"Thanks for the first aid and the drink, Mrs. Markham."

She came around the end of the bar and smiled up at him.

"Call me Sylvia."

"I will if you'll call me Keith."

"Okay, it's a deal. Thanks for bringing my kids home. They're always going through some phase or other and right now it's playing detective. They sneak out at night to detect things. If you see them, shoo them home, please."

"Sure thing. We single parents have to stick together."

As the door closed behind him, Keith reflected that Sylvia Markham was a very attractive woman. He was still reflecting on that when he went through his own front door to find Sunny clutching a drink and tapping her foot angrily. He started guiltily. He had forgotten all about Sunny. She stood up and set her drink on the glass coffee table with a click.

"Where the hell have you been?" she cried angrily.

He held up his bandaged hand. "Getting some first aid."

"I see. Those brats belong to a cute little nurse."

"Sunny, I wasn't gone ten minutes. What are you so angry about?"

"Ten minutes can be a long time, Keith."

Keith spoke pacifically. "All I did was take the kids home. Their mother saw that my hand was bleeding and insisted on rendering first aid."

"It doesn't take ten minutes to stick a bandage on."

"Don't you think this is a little silly? Sylvia asked me to have a drink and we chatted a few minutes."

"What does her husband do for a living?" Sunny demanded.

"She's not married," Keith answered incautiously.

"There!"

"What do you mean, *there*?" Keith asked impatiently. "She's just moved in and we hadn't met before. I told you that we chatted."

"And she let you know that she's a poor little woman all alone in the world and she needs a big strong man to help her hang the pictures. I'll bet you promised to go back tomorrow and fix the lawnmower or something."

Keith took her in his arms and kissed her ear. She allowed him to maneuver her to the couch.

"No, I didn't," he said softly. "She's just a nice little woman who happened to move in next door. She's not at all like you."

Sunny let him cajole her out of her jealousy and into a sexy mood. She unbuttoned his shirt and presently he unzipped her dress, unhooked her strapless bra, and buried his face in her bosom.

It was at that moment that Lindsay tiptoed to the front door, slipped through and closed it noiselessly behind her. There was only one lamp lighted in the living room so she was almost across the entry to the foot of the stairs when a glance showed her Keith and Sunny on the couch. She grinned broadly and swerved into the room.

"Hi, Dad," she said cheerfully. "Having fun?"

Keith jerked his head up and turned to his daughter, pulling his shirt together and trying to shield Sunny from Lindsay's eyes.

"Lindsay!" he exclaimed.

After one horrified, furious look at Lindsay, Sunny clutched her sundress to her chest and rushed from the room.

Lindsay called after her, "Don't go, lady. I'm going to bed now. I won't bother you any more."

"Lindsay." Even as he said it, Keith wished he could think of something else to say.

Lindsay put her hand over her mouth and tried to look contrite. "I guess you and the lady were just going to bed, too. Sorry I mentioned it."

Keith's suspicions had been roused. "Are you drunk?"

Lindsay shook her head. "No, Daddy. I had a couple of beers but I'm not drunk."

"Where have you been? Who were you with?"

Keith was on his feet by then, buttoning his shirt. He had seldom felt more foolish.

Lindsay gave him a reproachful look. "You can't expect me to tattle on my friends. Listen, you're a man of the world and I'm a girl of the world. I mean, we're all adults here. So you go ahead with what you were doing. I'll just tippy-toe up to my room and leave you to it."

"Yes, I certainly think you'd better go up to your room, young lady."

"You're mad at me, aren't you, Daddy?"

"No, I'm not mad. I'm disappointed. Go on. We'll talk about it in the morning."

"Yes, you are mad. You always call me 'young lady' when you're mad."

"Lindsay," Keith began only to be interrupted by Sunny.

She came into the room with her dress back in place and her hair freshly combed.

"I'd like to go home, now, Keith," she said.

Keith barely glanced at her, still focused on his daughter and her misbehavior.

"Yes," he said inattentively, "of course, Sunny."

He began to fish for his car keys. Not finding them in any of his pockets, he turned to the couch and began to probe the cushions.

"Did you lose something?" Lindsay inquired, brightly helpful.

"My keys. Sunny, did you see what I did..."

Sunny picked them up from the coffee table and handed them to him.

"Oh, that's right, I gave them to you, didn't I? Okay, ready?"

"Quite ready," she said icily, picking up her purse.

"Okay." He looked at Lindsay. "Will you be all right while I drive Sunny home?"

"I can call a cab, Keith," Sunny said through gritted teeth.

"I'll be okay, Dad. I'll just mix myself a little toddy for the body and when you get back we can have a little snort together."

"Lindsay, don't you dare touch that liquor cabinet while I'm gone. You've had more than enough already."

"I'm just kidding."

Sunny swept to the door and on outside.

Lindsay gestured after her. "I think the lady's ready to go," she suggested.

"I'll be right back," Keith said, worriedly.

He went out the front door and Lindsay followed him to lean over the porch rail as he and Sunny got into the convertible and began to back down the driveway.

"Hard to port, mate," she called. "Now, right rudder. Full speed astern. Port your helm, mister, lively now."

Keith stopped the car and got out.

"I think you'd better come with me," he said.

Lindsay was quite agreeable; she was having a fine time. Keith steered her into the back seat. Sunny was stonily silent as he backed out onto the street and headed down the hill toward Siskiyou Boulevard.

"You forgot your manners," Lindsay told him. "You didn't introduce me to the lady."

Keith shot a look at Sunny. "I didn't forget. I don't think the lady wants to know either one of us right now."

"It's all my fault," Lindsay mourned. "She liked you just fine before I came home. I'm sorry, lady. If I'd known you and my dad were getting it on, I would have stayed at Sue's tonight."

"Lindsay! That's enough." He was beginning to find the situation funny but he didn't want to offend Sunny more than she was already offended and he didn't want to encourage his daughter in her bratty behavior.

CHAPTER 16

Sunny flounced out of the car as soon as Keith stopped in front of her apartment house. She was inside almost before Keith could even think about going to the door with her. Lindsay began to laugh and flipped over the seat to sit beside him. She turned on the radio, tuned it to a raucous rock station and began to gyrate to the beat of the music.

"Are you going to share the joke?" Keith asked, as he pulled away from the curb and headed back home.

"I was just thinking how funny the world is. Don't you think it's a funny world?"

Keith turned the radio down.

"Yes. I sure do. Now, young lady, where were you tonight and what have you been drinking?"

"There you go again," Lindsay said sadly. "Now you're mad at me again."

They drove past the nearly empty parking lot of a nightclub where a group of young men were getting into a van with their musical instruments. Lindsay got up onto her knees and whistled ribaldly, waving when they turned to look. They grinned and waved.

"Hey, baby," one of them called.

"Let's party, mama," another one shouted.

Keith glared at his daughter. "Sit down and behave yourself."

Lindsay sat down and turned to her father. "Daddy, did you see that guy in the green shirt? His jeans sure fit nice. Doesn't it just blow your butt off when you see a guy in nice-fitting jeans? I mean a girl. For you, of course. But guys in tight jeans just freak me out. If they've got good asses, I mean. Who cares how his jeans fit, if a guy hasn't got a good..."

Keith interrupted her. "I know what you mean," he said dryly. "I wish you would try to remember that you're not in the girls' locker room and clean up your mouth a little for your father."

"Okay, Pop. Let's not go home yet. Let's find someone to party with."

"I think you'd better sleep it off, my child."

"Sleep?" Lindsay was incredulous. "I'm not going to sleep as long as I feel this good. Nope, I'm going to enjoy myself."

Keith turned into his driveway and parked. Lindsay hopped out of the car and began to

224

dance wildly, playing an air guitar and singing at the top of her voice. Keith got out of the car and went to her tiredly.

"Lindsay! Be quiet. People are trying to sleep."

"Dance with me. You haven't danced with me for a long time."

She stopped dancing and playing her air guitar.

"I'll play something slow for you, because you're always saying you're getting old."

She began to hum and Keith allowed her to get him dancing. Then she began to sing again, although not raucously. Sylvia Markham stuck her head out her upstairs window.

"Hello," she called softly. "We're really having an exciting night, aren't we?"

"Lindsay, stop that. Be still." Keith stopped dancing and looked up at Sylvia. Lindsay kept dancing but looked around until she located Sylvia.

"Hi," she called cheerily. "Would you like to dance? I'll play my air guitar and sing and you and Dad can dance. My dad dances real good."

"Yes, I see he does," Sylvia replied politely.

"Are you going to introduce me to this lady?" Lindsay asked Keith in a stage whisper.

"Sylvia, this is my daughter, Lindsay. Lindsay, this is our new neighbor, Mrs.

Markham."

"I'm extremely pleased to meet you, Mrs. Markham."

"The pleasure's mine, Lindsay."

"I'm sorry we disturbed you," Keith apologized. "She's a little exuberant. I'll take her inside. Good night again."

"Good night."

"I'm not going in..." Lindsay began.

Keith picked her up and slung her over his shoulder. She tilted her head to look up at Sylvia.

"Good night," Lindsay called to her. Then, in a stage whisper, she asked her father, "Why don't you make out with her instead of with the blond lady? I like Mrs. Markham."

Keith set her on her feet at the foot of the stairs. She sat on the bottom step and looked at him seriously.

"How come you always say you're getting old? You carried me just as easily as Greg does. And you sure didn't seem old when I came in tonight. No, you were acting pretty young then."

"Who's Greg?"

"A guy I know. His jeans fit pretty nice. Not as nice as Pat's but nice."

"Will you quit that? What's Greg's last name?"

"Nope. You think I was out with him tonight and you want to burn him."

Keith pulled her to her feet.

"Come on, let's get you to bed."

"Okay, I'll race you to the top."

Lindsay ran up the stairs. Keith turned off the living room lamp and locked the front door, then walked upstairs. Lindsay waited for him on the landing and kissed him goodnight. He watched doubtfully as she went into her room. She picked up her battered old penguin and danced with it. Keith went into his room and was emptying his pockets, putting his keys, wallet, and so forth on his dresser when Lindsay knocked on his door.

"Come in."

Lindsay opened the door and spoke earnestly. "It's okay if you're mad at me because I've been naughty and I deserve it. But don't be mad at Greg. Greg wasn't even there tonight. I suppose he's going to be mad at me, too, because I went to that party without him."

"What party?"

"I can't tell you that. I told you I don't rat on my friends."

"Tell me this. Was it just some kind of beer bust with your friends?"

"You know that frat house -- the one that's always in some kind of trouble?"

"You were at a frat house?" Keith was getting more upset by the minute.

"Sure. They were having a party. They were

having, like, nameless orgies."

Keith grabbed her by the shoulders and shook her a little. "Tell me exactly what happened."

Lindsay twisted out of his grasp. "Daddy, I'm just teasing you. We weren't at the frat house. I got invited once, though. But I didn't go."

"Lindsay, will you stop playing games and tell me where you were and what you did tonight?"

She smiled diabolically. "What's the matter? Afraid your sweet little daughter is an easy lay?"

"No, of course not." Keith was appalled by her bluntness and that she appeared to know exactly what to say to rile him.

"Sure you are. There's something I want to know. How come men chase easy lays but they don't want their own women to be easy lays?"

"I don't think that's quite fair, Lindsay. There used to be a double standard like that but I think it's pretty much a thing of the past."

"Do you really care about that lady we took home tonight?"

"I'm not going to discuss her with you."

"Uh huh. That's what I thought. She's an easy lay."

Keith was acutely uncomfortable and very upset. "Will you quit saying that? Go to bed and sleep it off. We'll talk in the morning."

"Okay, Pop. But you might think it over."

She went out and closed his door behind her. He was in bed with the light off when there was another knock on his door.

"Go to bed, Lindsay. Go to sleep," he called.

She knocked again and he sat up resignedly and turned his bedside lamp on. "Come in."

Lindsay came in, wearing her pajamas and carrying her penguin. He hastily pulled his toes up as she plopped down on the end of his bed.

"Daddy, is it true that men are very easy to arouse -- like by women wearing tight sweaters or short shorts? Sexually, I mean."

Keith bit his tongue. Then he decided to try shock tactics. Maybe if he was as frank as she, it would embarrass her enough to leave him alone. "I thought you might mean that," he said. "Yes, it's true. That's why I don't like for you to wear them. It isn't safe, sometimes, and it isn't fair to tease the boys."

"Then why is it okay for boys to wear tight jeans or shorts? Girls get aroused too."

"It's easier to arouse a man's passion than a woman's. Men are also more prone to frustration."

She nodded wisely. "Blue balls."

Keith put a pillow over his face. "Lindsay," he wailed, muffled by the pillow.

"Did I shock you again? I'm sorry, but I need to know these things. Greg says that if men get aroused but not satisfied..."

Keith put the pillow down. "Do you mean to tell me that you and this Greg character discuss these things?"

Lindsay was surprised. "Sure. Didn't you and Mother talk about them? Don't you talk about them with the blond lady?"

"Look, I don't think it's any of your business what your mother and I discussed or what Sunny and I discuss."

"I suppose not. Sorry, Pop. I guess you're pretty frustrated tonight, huh? It's interesting that it makes you cranky. It makes me cranky, too. Heredity, I suppose." She looked at him thoughtfully. "I don't think men are really easier to arouse because I don't think anyone could be easier to arouse than I am. Or more prone to frustration. Of course, I don't have to contend with blue balls."

Keith tried to speak casually. "You are still frustrated, then?"

"So far. I'm not an easy lay. But it's getting harder all the time. But you know all about that, don't you?" Suddenly she laughed. "You know, I thought you were celibate all this time. Until tonight. It's sort of nice to know you have the same problems as I do. But I think you ought to get married again." She slid off the bed and went to the door. "You shouldn't screw around with the easy lays too much. You might get a social disease or AIDS or something."

Lindsay went out and shut his door behind her again. Keith sat and stared after her, too outraged to speak.

The next morning, after a mostly sleepless night, Keith went out to the back yard and dug in the garden, thinning the clumps of iris and shasta daisies and other perennial plants. He usually sought the garden when he was troubled and mostly it brought him calm and peace and healing. That morning the magic worked as usual, helping him put Lindsay's peccadilloes in perspective and restoring his sense of humor to some degree. Even so, he knew he must have a very serious talk with his daughter.

About eight o'clock she came out the back door, wearing a demure blue dress and carrying two glasses of orange juice. He propped his spade against a tree trunk and accepted the proffered glass of juice. They both sat on the grass and sipped, eyeing each other a little warily.

"Good morning, Daddy. Isn't it a glorious day?"

"I've always said you're a bright girl."

"What do you mean?"

"I mean it's very astute of you to wear that dress instead of shorts or tight jeans this morning. Evidently, my psychology is an open book to you."

Lindsay smiled ruefully. "I'm sorry it's so obvious."

"I'm sure," Keith said dryly. Then he smiled at her. "Don't you have a headache or anything this morning?"

"Not a single throb," she said.

"It's nice to be young," Keith sighed.

"About last night -- I'm really sorry."

"What exactly are you sorry for, Lindsay? Sorry you got drunk? Sorry you came home past your curfew? Sorry you were rude? Or just sorry you got caught?"

"Let's see." Lindsay frowned as she concentrated on getting her answers in the right order. "I'm not very sorry I got drunk except you're mad at me for it. I'm sorry if I was rude; I didn't mean to be. I'm sorry you caught me breaking curfew. What else?"

"That about covers it. We can write off most of it as the result of the booze. But the drinking will have to be dealt with. Any ideas?"

"I hate it when you do that. Make me think up my own punishment."

"You thought up the behavior, it seems reasonable to me that you should think up a way to cope with it."

"You could spank me. That would clear the

air and get it over with right away."

"I think you're a little elderly for spanking. Besides, that would be too easy. Maybe we ought to try making the punishment fit the transgressions."

"You know, Daddy, you never did actually forbid me to get drunk," she offered hopefully.

"Nice try but you won't get out of it that way. You know that drinking is unacceptable behavior for teenagers. I think that for the next two weeks you'd better be home by nine."

"Daddy. Nine o'clock's for little kids. I won't even be able to go to the movies if I have to be home by nine."

"I know. I also think we'd better keep you home from say, two to five in the afternoons. That'll cut out parties at the lake and other tempting situations."

"It isn't fair," Lindsay exclaimed. "No one else has this big a deal made out of getting a little wasted one time."

"Two things. I'm not raising anyone but you. And it isn't so much the getting wasted that bothers me, it's the not being sorry. This will give you a chance to see that getting wasted has some ill effects."

"Not from the booze, though, from you!"

"It's like this," Keith said, reasonably. "I can't stop you from doing anything you want to do. I mean that quite literally. If you decide to do something, there is nothing I can do to stop you. You could find a way."

He looked at her questioningly and she reluctantly nodded her head.

"All I can do is teach," he continued. "I can set up artificial consequences in the hope that you'll refrain from outright defiance until you're old enough to see the natural consequences for yourself."

Lindsay nodded again, acknowledging the truth he was setting forth but not wanting to.

"I don't want to say this next part," he went on, "but after last night, I guess I'd better. It embarrasses me to talk about sex with you. I assumed that you would learn what you needed to know in school but I can't dodge it any longer."

"I don't see what's so embarrassing about it, but, yes, we learned about the little polliwogs and eggs."

"They're still showing that moldy old film?"

"You mean they showed it to you?"

"Yeah, we had to have notes from our parents saying it was okay for us to watch it."

"How humiliating."

"Yeah. Okay, you know the mechanics. Did anyone talk about values or morals?"

"Not really. Miss Carlson talked a lot about

diseases and protection is all."

"Birth control?"

"Sure. IUDs, condoms, the pill, coitus interruptus..."

Keith broke into her catalog. "Okay. All right, the aftermath of the pleasures of sex are often painful. What we have to try to do is make sure that no one is being hurt. Physically, emotionally, spiritually. And that means not only yourself and your partner, but the people close to you, as well as the child who might result."

Keith was glad to see that Lindsay was listening carefully. He was still greatly embarrassed but he forged on manfully.

"You talked a lot last night about easy lays. It may look to an easy lay as if she isn't being hurt, but she's allowing her body to be turned into a dirty joke and that's got to have a terrible effect on her self-image."

"I understand that," Lindsay interjected. "I figured that out for myself a long time ago or I'd probably be easy by now. But what about the guys? Doesn't it have the same effect on their self-image? How come it's okay for guys but not for girls?"

"To tell you the truth, I never thought about it. My generation of guys didn't. We divided the girls into nice girls and easy girls. We screwed the easy ones and married the nice ones. I don't know what effect it had on us."

"I've got psychology next year. Maybe I'll research it and write a term paper about it."

"God help me." Keith hesitated then decided to get it all off his chest, now that he had started. "One more thing. I hope that you'll wait for marriage but if you decide to have sex before you're married, don't bring me any babies. I won't raise them for you."

"I won't bring you any babies, Dad, but I want to know: if I did, would you disown me? Send me out into the snow to starve? Or what?"

"Nothing you could do would make me love you any less, Lindsay. But I won't shoulder the responsibility for your actions. I would do what I could to help you, short of raising the child myself."

"Okay, I understand." She started to get up but Keith put a hand on her arm.

"One last thing -- if you can't wait, don't pretend it's a sudden, irresistible impulse in the back seat of a car somewhere. Plan for it so you won't get any ugly surprises."

Lindsay nodded solemnly and stood up. She leaned over and kissed him on the forehead. At the back door she turned and grinned at him.

"Okay, Pop. I'll lay in a supply of rubbers and use my bedroom."

She was inside with the door closed before he

recovered enough to speak. He shook his head, glad of her spunk but a little apprehensive of where it might lead her.

CHAPTER 17

That summer was a happy one. Keith and Lindsay remained close, even through the trials of late puberty. They also grew close to the Markham family. They both enjoyed the little kids' antics and they both appreciated Sylvia's sterling qualities. Keith didn't appreciate Scott so much, especially when Lindsay and he dated some. It didn't seem to come to anything, much to his relief. Mostly they shared the same group activities -- boating at the lake, going to 4-H camp as teen counselors, swimming at Jackson WellSprings and volunteering to work in the Tree of Life Garden. About once a week the two families got together for a backyard cookout. Fortunately, Alma and Sylvia became friends, exchanging recipes and helping one another manage their households.

As a real estate agent, Sylvia could usually set her own hours but occasionally she had to be away when Geoffrey and Allison were home. Alma was glad for them to come to her at those times and she baked cookies for them as she had for Lindsay and her own children. Lindsay treated them like the younger siblings she had sometimes longed for but never had, getting a kick out of their conversation and playing games with them.

Keith admired Sylvia and enjoyed her company. She was a gutsy lady who asked no help from any man and spoke her mind without fear or favor. Scott looked on with disapproval when Keith and Sylvia began to date but Lindsay was delighted and dropped lots of hints that she would welcome Sylvia as a step-mother. She pointed out that their house was large enough to meld the two families and Alma would almost certainly stay on as housekeeper and what fun it was to have Allison and Geoffrey around and that she and Scott would be going off to college in a couple of years and Keith needed more family to keep him company. Keith found her hints comical and laughed them off. Much as he liked Sylvia, he had no wish to marry again, nor even to date her exclusively. He was perfectly satisfied with things as they were.

For her part, Sylvia carefully concealed from Keith her deep love for him and her hope that one day he would ask her to marry him. She knew intuitively that if he guessed how much she cared for him, he would withdraw from the relationship. She knew that he was involved with other women and she was both hurt and jealous. Even so, she never tried to find out who they were or even how many there were. Scott occasionally remonstrated with her, telling her that she was allowing herself to be used and made a fool of. Always she told him to mind his own business. Keith had never made her any promises and she had never asked for any.

Then, without any warning, Keith found his comfortable life beginning to unravel. It was early autumn and the kids had just gone back to school when he got a phone call one afternoon. He was at his office, working on an idea he'd suddenly got for a workman's cottage. He'd been thinking about Merrilee and the cottage where they had spent that summer so long ago. It was just like thousands of its kind all over Oregon, hell, he thought, all over the country, probably all over the world. It was small and cramped and dingy and unhandy. Poverty, or comparative poverty, was hard enough to endure without one's housing emphasizing it. He'd been contemplating the changes that would have made that cottage more comfortable, both physically and emotionally, wondering if the time had come to donate some time and money to building a prototype model of an inexpensive but efficient and cheerful home. When the phone rang, it took him a minute to orient himself.

"Vi Devereaux? What the hell does she want? Okay, Stan, put her through."

Keith couldn't imagine what Vi Devereaux wanted. He seldom saw her and he had never pretended to like her.

"Keith," she cooed, "how have you been? I haven't seen you for an age. Are you in seclusion?"

"Just about. Keeping my nose to the grindstone and my shoulder to the wheel. How about you?"

"I'm fine. I missed you at the Burns' open house last night."

"I couldn't make it." Keith was more puzzled than ever. What possible difference could it make to Vi Devereaux if he went to the Burns' open house or not?

She laughed her malicious little tinkling laugh that always set his teeth on edge.

"A little bird told me that you and Virginia had other plans."

He'd been seeing Virginia Collins who was a divorcée with more spare time and money than were good for her. He'd known she and Vi were friends but couldn't see why Vi should take any particular interest in their plans.

"Vi, I'm working against a deadline right now. Maybe we can have lunch or something sometime next week."

"Maybe. Listen, Keith, I wasn't sure if you knew it or not but Virginia's in the hospital in Medford."

Keith was startled. He and Virginia had spent the last weekend together at a bed and breakfast near Newport over on the coast. They'd had a pleasant time touring various wineries and driving around looking at the old victorian homes. They had gone to a semi-professional little theatre production of "Arsenic and Old Lace" that had been fun. Virginia had been fine when he'd taken her home Sunday night.

"In the hospital?" he repeated, surprised and puzzled. Vi didn't sound right to be giving news of a friend's hospitalization; she sounded smug. "What happened? Did she have an accident?"

"It must have been," Vi said, sounding amused as well as smug. "Knowing Virginia, I didn't think she'd tell you but I thought you'd want to know."

Keith had had enough of Vi's silly game, whatever it was. "Yes, I do. Thanks for calling."

He cradled the handpiece of the phone without waiting for Vi to respond. He stopped long enough to tell Stan, the receptionist, that he didn't know how long he would be gone. He drove to a florist and bought a big pot of deep pink cyclamen then to the Medford hospital.

Keith found Virginia lying in a private room, looking pale and wan, listlessly watching TV. When Keith entered the room looking concerned, she gave him a big smile and flicked the TV off. He set the flowers on the over-the-bed table, kissed her cheek, and took one of her hands in his.

"What happened? Vi Devereaux just called to tell me you'd had some kind of accident?"

"I guess that's as good a way to put it as any," Virginia said with a small, unamused laugh.

"What are you talking about, Virginia? What happened?"

"I tried to tell you last weekend but we were having such a good time that I didn't want to spoil it."

"Tell me what? You knew you were going to have an accident?"

She groped for the bed control and raised herself to a more upright position.

"I had an abortion this morning, Keith."

He dropped her hand as if he'd suddenly found it unclean. She smiled again, shrugging her shoulders.

"I found out I was pregnant and I knew you didn't want to get married. So, the only thing to do was to get rid of it."

"You killed my baby?" Keith was outraged.

Virginia was astonished. "I thought you'd

want -- It wasn't -- I didn't -- I terminated a pregnancy. I have the right to do that."

Keith was coldly furious. "You had no right. You had no right. You didn't want him but I did. You had no right to take my baby's life."

"Keith. I didn't know. I thought..." Virginia's voice trailed off. She had begun to see the vast dimensions of the mistake she had made.

"You thought I wanted you to murder my child?"

"It wasn't a child," Virginia protested. "It wasn't a baby at all, just a fetus. It was only eight weeks. It was just a fetus!"

Keith turned and walked out without another word, without a backward glance.

The day that had been warm and sunny in the Rogue River Valley was cool and cloudy up in the mountains. It was dark when Keith knocked on Jazzy and Lora's front door and had turned downright cold as a light skiff of snow fell.

Lora came to the door. "Keith. Come in, come in."

"Lora."

Keith both looked and felt cold and bleak. As he went in, he saw Jazzy sprawled out in an easy chair in front of the fire, toasting his stocking feet. Lora shut the door and put her arms around Keith. He laid his head on her shoulder, holding her close to him. After a few moments, Lora gently pulled away from him and guided him into the living room to a chair opposite Jazzy. Jazzy, alarmed by Keith's demeanor, jumped up to get him a shot of whiskey. Lora took it from him and handed it to Keith.

"Drink it," she said. "It'll do you good. You are nearly frozen."

There were several youngsters of various ages scattered around the room, some watching TV, some reading or playing video games on their laptops.

"Kids," Lora said, "would you turn off the TV and go do your homework in the dining room?"

One of the girls looked up at her, "My homework's done."

"That's fine," Lora said. "But take your games and books into the dining room anyway. Okay?"

The kids cast curious glances at Keith but they all went out.

Keith took a sip of the whiskey and put the glass down.

"What is it, Keith?" Jazzy asked.

"I..." Keith couldn't say it yet. These were his oldest and, since Kurt's death, his dearest friends. They knew all about him and loved him anyway. He found a corner of his mind functioning enough to wonder why they loved him. He was finding out some things about himself that made him feel pretty unlovable. "Can I stay here a couple of days?"

"Sure. As long as you want," Jazzy said.

"Thanks."

"Keith," Lora put her hand on his arm. "Is anything wrong with Lindsay?"

"She's fine. She doesn't know I'm here."

"I'll call her and tell her you're going to stay a couple of days. Okay?"

Keith nodded and stared into the flames of the fireplace, glancing up at Jazzy now and then. Lora came back and sat on the raised hearth and looked worriedly at Keith.

"Lindsay says stay as long as you want, Keith," she said. "She and Alma will take care of everything. And she said she'd let Alicia know you won't be at the office for a couple of days."

Keith flicked a tiny smile at Lora, "Thanks."

"I'm going to put you in the south room. I'll see to making up the bed." Lora stood up but Keith put out a hand toward her.

"I'd rather use one of the cabins, if you don't mind," he said.

Lora glanced at Jazzy for guidance and he nodded.

"Okay, if you'd rather," she said.

"I'd rather. Does it matter which?"

"Number ten, I think. I'll go check it."

"Don't bother," Keith said. "It'll be fine."

Lora put her hand on his shoulder and he covered it with his own.

"You know I'm going to check it," she said, with a smile.

She went to the kitchen and took her jacket off the hook as she passed through the back porch. As soon as she came back, Keith bade her and Jazzy good night and went to the cabin. It was a wonderful blend of modern comfort and authentic-seeming rusticity, built of logs with a stone fireplace.

It was nearly dawn and the fire Lora had lighted the night before had burned out. Keith had opened the curtains and was lying in bed, staring out the window, as he had been all night. The pre-dawn light dimmed the stars and brought the other cabins and the trees into shadowy relief. About seven Lora knocked on the door and Keith hastily dragged on his jeans and shrugged into his shirt.

"Come in," he called.

Lora came in with a tray: a plate of hot food for him and a pot of coffee and two mugs. "I brought you some breakfast," she said, with a smile.

Keith took the tray from her and set it on the table. "You shouldn't have gone to all this bother, Lora."

"It was no bother," she replied, sitting at the table and motioning for him to sit also. She poured them each a cup of coffee and Keith picked up his fork and scooped up a bite of fried potatoes. Without tasting it, he put it back on his plate.

"I can't swallow food. I'm sorry," he said.

"Can't you share whatever this is? I can't bear to see you in so much pain. It'll help to talk it out. Like it did when Kurt was killed and when our baby died."

Keith looked her full in the face and responded to the love and concern he saw there. "It's happened again. It's like a nightmare that I can't get out of. That I shouldn't get out of because it's my fault."

"Tell me." Lora's voice was soft but there was command in it.

"When we started this project, your dude ranch, Jazzy talked to me like a Dutch uncle but I wouldn't listen. I wouldn't listen. And now another baby is dead and it's my fault."

"Keith..."

He interrupted. "Wait. I expect you know that I've been pretty promiscuous since Phyllis left me."

Lora nodded, keeping her face neutral.

"I got one of my women pregnant. And she thought I wouldn't want the baby and had an abortion. I didn't even know she was pregnant until afterwards."

"Oh, no," Lora whispered, the pain of her own child's death stabbing at her.

"Pretty ironic, isn't it? There's you and Jazzy wanting a baby. There's me wanting a son. And she has an abortion."

Keith couldn't just sit still; he went to the fireplace and built a fire. When it was burning satisfactorily, he went back and sat at the table. He held his coffee mug as if he was trying to absorb its warmth.

CHAPTER 18

Keith stayed on at the cabin for several days. He spent a great deal of time hiking in the mountains, drawing strength from the woods. The Janowskis' friendship helped him to heal as both Lora and Jazzy spent hours talking with him, both separately and together. He was sitting in his cabin one evening, watching the pine logs pop and sizzle as they burned, thinking that it was time he went home and faced life again. The phone rang and he eyed it distastefully. He let it ring twice more before he picked it up.

Phyllis sat in her small, shabbily-furnished apartment, a glass of ice and scotch in front of her, a cell phone in her hand. She sipped as she listened to Keith's phone ring and nearly choked when he answered.

"Kovacek."

"Keith. You don't recognize my voice, do you?"

He didn't, at first. "I'm sorry," he began and then it hit him. "Phyllis?"

"How are you, Keith?"

"How did you find me?" He wasn't outright hostile but he was far from cordial. To have Phyllis pop up in his life at the present time was pretty close to the top of a list of things he would least like to happen.

"A woman at your house gave me the number. New wife?"

"Housekeeper. What do you want?"

Phyllis was irritated at his tone. Surely, after so many years he could be civil, but apparently not. If he could be curt, so could she. "Lindsay."

"No."

"You can hardly stop me from seeing her. She's my daughter, too."

"No. Not after all these years."

"I want her to spend her birthday and Christmas with me. Maybe next summer."

"No."

"You can't just keep saying 'no.' I'm coming next week and I'll bring her back here with me for the holidays."

"Where's 'here'?"

"Denver."

"Listen," Keith said, his voice cold and hard, "you can't have her. You ran out on her when she was three years old. She thinks you're dead."

"Dead? How could you do that to her?"

"It was your idea. Remember?"

Phyllis took a couple of swallows of scotch. "I remember. But I didn't suppose you'd really do it. I didn't know you hated me so much."

"I don't hate you. But you're not going to take Lindsay."

"Listen, Keith, if it's any comfort to you, Roger and I split up two years after we left Ashland together. There hasn't been a day in the last thirteen years that I haven't regretted leaving. Lindsay is all I have."

"Then you have nothing because Lindsay is not yours."

He replaced the receiver on the phone cradle, pulled on his coat and went outside to walk himself so tired he could stop replaying the conversation over and over in his head. In Denver, Phyllis put her head down on the table and sobbed.

Keith went back home the next morning, leaving Lora and Jazzy wondering what in the world had happened to galvanize him into such sudden movement. He spent the day seeing Lindsay's teachers and arranging for her to get and return her assignments by e-mail. He explained that he was obliged to take an extensive business trip and thought it would be good for Lindsay to see something of her native land. Then he went to the office and cleared his desk of as much as he could. Some work he packed into his briefcase as he talked to his partner.

"I don't know exactly how long I'll be gone, Alicia. Maybe two or three months."

"All right," she answered placidly.

"I'll be in touch about these plans and the other projects but I'm afraid I'm going to have to ask you to do the supervising. In fact, all the actual work."

She smiled at him. "That's okay. I can make up for taking maternity leave four times and leaving you to cover for me."

"Thanks, partner."

Keith smiled at her with real affection and respect. He gave her a quick peck on the cheek and then he was gone.

Lindsay was ecstatic when he picked her up after school and told her they would be going on an extended vacation, traveling all around. It puzzled her greatly because it seemed out of character for her normally methodical father to take off in a whirlwind but she was so glad to be invited along that she tabled her curiosity. Alma was both puzzled and disapproving. She knew that something had happened to Keith but she couldn't guess what it was. However, she agreed to stay on and take care of the home front, especially Pepper. In his rush to be out of reach of Phyllis and any legal machinery she might invoke, Keith had no thought to spare for Sylvia or any of the Markham family. By midnight he and Lindsay were packed; by seven-seventeen the next morning they were in the Mercedes, backing down the drive.

"This is the life," Lindsay remarked as they climbed up out of the Rogue River Valley, following the river east, against the current. "No school, no homework, no hassles."

"Wait a minute, now. I promised Ms. Swearingen faithfully that you'd have all your assignments finished and e-mailed according to the schedule your teachers gave me."

"That's okay," Lindsay said airily. "I'll get them done. But this is great; no schedules to keep, no daily grind. Dad, you're like, awesome."

Keith grinned at her. "Like, thanks."

"You know what we should do?" Lindsay asked and answered without waiting for her father to speak. "I just read a book called *Blue Highways*. This guy that wrote it, William Least-Heat Moon -- isn't that a name for you? Anyway, he took off on some kind of pilgrimage or something and decided to stay off the interstate highways and travel only on the secondary ones, the ones that are blue on the maps. He said that's the only way you get to see the real America, all the regional differences and special things. Everything's the same on the interstate system, just a bunch of food and gas franchises everywhere you go. So that's what we should do, stay on the blue highways."

"Sounds sensible. I read that book when it first came out. I've seen enough airports and interstates to last me the rest of my life."

"This highway we're on now, it's a blue highway, isn't it?"

"Yup. It used to be a major highway but since they finished the interstate network, most of the traffic sticks to that."

Lindsay loved to travel. Every new sight enraptured her, every new experience thrilled her. Keith, now that he had her out of her mother's reach, without even a cell phone along, relaxed and enjoyed his daughter's company to the full. She wanted to stop and read every historical marker and take in every roadside attraction. He usually indulged her.

The first stop they made was at the Rogue River Gorge. Keith had seen the gorge many times but it was new to Lindsay and she reacted with a delighted wonder that her father felt was a good omen for their sojourn. The depth of the chasm wasn't all that much but the river ran deep, swift and unforgiving. A chain link fence separated them from the brink, which detracted from the feeling of being connected to elemental forces, but which both father and daughter inwardly approved of. Anyone who fell into the roiling, frothing water at the bottom of the gorge would almost certainly be dashed to death on the boulders or drowned in the current.

An ancient monarch of the forest had fallen across the gorge and was overgrown with moss, very picturesque and rather unsettling, as it suggested a bridge at the same time that it looked far too wet and slippery to cross safely. When she had absorbed as much of the turbulent grandeur as she could, Lindsay walked upstream a few rods to where the river had sculpted swirling bowls into the living rock of the riverbank. She squatted and ran her fingers over the smooth inner surface of one of the bowls, marveling at the forces at work over thousands of years to carve so deeply and beautifully.

Keith took a route across the lava flows and cones of central Oregon, through the forested mountains of eastern Oregon, up onto the arid plateau on the northwest side of the Blue Mountains. Lindsay was disappointed that they hadn't thought of taking the trip in time for the Pendleton Roundup. They spent a day crossing Idaho, following the exquisitely lovely Clearwater River with its ranks of evergreens covering the mountainsides. They kept to the northern tier of states all across the continent. Both of them were awe-struck at the Mississippi

River, thinking of the history and folklore evoked by it, although they agreed that the Columbia was just as good and the Snake better.

They avoided the cities as much as possible, neither of them caring for the jammed-up feeling of crowds and dense traffic. Lindsay did most of her homework in the car as they traveled, reading and using her laptop computer to write essays and term papers.

Keith was never very happy as a passenger but he recognized that Lindsay needed experience so he allowed her to drive now and then, much to her delight. At Columbus, they decided that as long as they were within reach, they ought to see New York City. They spent a couple of days taking bus tours to see things they weren't much interested in then moved on to Massachusetts and Rhode Island, most of which they found fascinating. They trekked on up to Maine, feeling at home again in the woods and among the people.

For Thanksgiving they crossed over to Canada and to Prince Edward Island. From the time she graduated from Little Golden Books and *Hiawatha* to read for herself, Lindsay had fallen in love with L.M. Montgomery's books, especially the "Anne" stories. She was thrilled to be where Anne had lived and to see the places Anne had loved. Keith enjoyed Lindsay's happiness and found the island a beautiful place in its own right. After a few days, they crossed back to the mainland and made their leisurely way south.

There were a lot of interesting places to see and historical sites to visit and father and daughter took the time to see most of them. Lindsay wished that there were more that were not tied to either the Revolutionary War or the Civil War. Keith wished there was less Euro-American chauvinism and more of the viewpoints of the Indian peoples and non-European immigrants. By the time they finished with Williamsburg, they were both surfeited with history so they went to Tennessee and hit all the country music hot spots. More than the hot spots, though, they both enjoyed the loveliness of the countryside.

Lindsay was a little puzzled when her dad headed almost due west from Memphis. They had talked of going to New Orleans but Keith seemed to have lost interest in the city. He was very quiet and seemed preoccupied. Lindsay began to worry that there was something wrong at home, maybe with Alma or Pepper. Or maybe something was wrong at the office, something Alicia couldn't handle.

Four days before Christmas they pulled into Denver. The city was decorated for the holidays and myriad tiny white lights sparkled from every tree, bush, building, and pole. Keith took a suite in one of the downtown hotels. He looked so strained and pale that Lindsay wondered for the first time if he was sick. The idea startled her. In common with most daughters who more or less idolize their fathers, she had never given any thought to the idea of her father being anything but strong and healthy. She curled up on the sofa and pretended to read a novel while surreptitiously watching Keith, who prowled around the suite restlessly. Finally, with an air of having come to a momentous decision, he sat in an easy chair across from the sofa.

"Lindsay," he said.

She gave him her full attention, surprised and apprehensive at his nervousness.

"Yes, Dad?"

He leaned toward her, elbows on knees. "Put your book down, will you? I have something to tell you."

"Okay." She put the book, splayed open, face down beside her.

"This is going to cause you pain," Keith said.

Lindsay was flabbergasted. This was a father she had not met before. She opened her mouth to protest but he held up his hand, palm outward and shook his head at her.

"It's going to hurt you, maybe a little, maybe

a lot. The original source of the pain I don't believe is my fault. But something I've done is going to make it worse and I want you to know how sorry I am before I tell you. Because I'm afraid that after I tell you, you'll turn away from me. I've always done my best for you, but in this I've failed you. I hope you'll try to underst..."

Lindsay interrupted. She was alarmed for him. She couldn't stand for him to look and talk like that. She uncurled herself and sat forward on the edge of the sofa.

"Daddy, it can't be as bad as that. You know I could never turn away from you. Even if you murdered someone. And I know you haven't done anything as bad as that."

Keith gave her an ironic, fleeting smile. "In a way I have murdered someone. Only now she's come back to life and I have to tell you about it."

Lindsay reached for his hand and he gave her fingers a gentle squeeze.

"Okay, tell me about it," she said.

"Remember when you were a little girl and you asked me where your mommy was?"

"And you told me she was dead."

"That's what I have to tell you, Lindsay. I lied to you. Your mother is not dead, she's very much alive."

Keith had worked himself up to a high pitch of inner turmoil and had been bracing himself for days to make this confession and bear whatever reproaches his daughter might fling at him.

"I know," she said, calmly and matter of factly, "Sue Pohl told me when I was in the first grade."

Keith was intensely relieved but, at the same time, he was nearly indignant that his angst had been for nothing. Sue Pohl had told his daughter his closely guarded secret ten years earlier. It was ludicrous. It was outrageous.

"You knew? And you never mentioned it?"

"I figured you had your reasons and I knew it was a sore subject. She hurt you pretty bad, didn't she?"

"It was bad," Keith conceded. He slumped back in his chair, eyeing his daughter curiously, trying to fit this reaction into his previous knowledge of her. "But it was a long time ago. I thought I'd nearly forgotten it until she called. She's here in Denver and she wants to see you."

Lindsay was alarmed. "So that's what this trip is all about. You didn't bring me here to leave me with her, did you?"

Keith sat up and smiled at her, but anxiety was still in his face and his voice. "No. No, this trip was to keep you out of town so she and her lawyer couldn't find you. I finally realized how unfair to you that was. Now it's up to you. See her or not. Whatever. It's not my decision."

"Then I don't have to live with her? Or stay with her?" Lindsay wanted to get her options completely clear.

"No. You don't have to spend any more time with her than you want to. I'll try not to interfere in any relationship you develop with her. But I have to tell you that I feel very threatened and I don't really want you to have a relationship with her. That's just my insecurity and you don't have to cater to it. I just wanted you to know so you can assess any weirdness I come up with."

Lindsay grinned at him affectionately. "And what's the cause of the weirdness you came up with before?"

"A little angelic-looking girl who used to do things like hose down the kitchen to put out imaginary fires."

They both laughed and suddenly they were standing, hugging each other fiercely, love washing over and through them in a moment that neither would ever forget.

CHAPTER 19

Keith called Phyllis and arranged for her to meet Lindsay at the hotel. Unsure exactly how she felt, Lindsay had wanted Keith to go with her but he demurred, thinking it best for mother and daughter to get acquainted without his presence. Phyllis was standing in the lobby when Lindsay got off the elevator. Both were ill at ease and nervous as they walked toward one another.

"Mother?" Lindsay was oddly surprised to find her mother so different from the woman in the photograph she had kept in her room for so many years.

"Lindsay." Whatever Phyllis had expected, she was just as surprised as Lindsay at the difference the years had wrought. The only thing she could see hadn't changed about Lindsay was her eyes. They were still deep brown, still honestly seeking, still warm and expressive. She threw her arms around her daughter and her heart contracted painfully as she felt Lindsay's complete lack of response. She stepped back and looked around.

"Where's your father?" she asked. "Isn't he coming down?"

"Daddy thought we'd rather be alone."

"Yes, of course. Keith was always thoughtful. Shall we find some place to sit?"

Lindsay led the way to a quiet corner, out of the main traffic lanes. They sat and gazed at one another in silence for a few moments. Phyllis spoke first.

"I've dreamed of this for years and now it's come, it's more awkward than I expected. You're not going to make it easy for me, are you?"

"I'm trying. But it's hard to believe that you just walked away. You hurt Daddy terribly, you know."

"Lindsay, don't judge me. You only know your father's side. You don't know mine."

"Okay, let's say you had a good reason for leaving. Let's say Daddy was cruel, he beat you or something horrible. I know he couldn't but let's just say that he did. For the sake of argument. That still leaves me. Even if you had good reasons to leave Daddy, why did you leave me? And stay away all these years?"

Phyllis felt as if Lindsay had struck her. She looked into her daughter's face and saw the gulf that she herself had put between the two of them.

"I can't make you understand, Lindsay.

Because I don't understand." Phyllis rose to her feet. "Let's go into the restaurant. Wouldn't you like something to drink?"

"If you would," Lindsay answered politely.

Phyllis chose a table in a quiet corner and the hostess handed them menus which they immediately laid aside. They sat in silence until the waiter came to take their order.

"Scotch on the rocks," Phyllis told him. "Make it a double. Lindsay?"

"Tea, please."

"Lemon or cream?" the waiter asked.

"Neither, thanks."

The waiter went.

"Keith's taught you nice manners," Phyllis said with a smile. "I'll give him that."

"You think Daddy's told me all about you and how you left us, don't you?"

"Hasn't he?"

"You don't know him very well. All my life he's told me that you loved me very much. He gave me some pictures of you -- beautiful pictures. I used to look in the mirror every morning to see if I was starting to look anything like you. I wanted to be beautiful like you so much."

The waiter brought their drinks and Phyllis immediately ordered another. Lindsay waited until he had gone before finishing her speech.

265

"Daddy has never said anything bad about you."

Phyllis nodded thoughtfully. "You think your father's pretty wonderful, don't you?"

"He has his faults. But, yes, I guess I do think he's pretty wonderful."

"So what did he say to explain what happened -- since I'm not dead? He did tell you I was dead, didn't he?"

"He said you fell out of love with him and in love with another man. That's all he said about you."

Phyllis' face twisted with pain. Both women were glad when the waiter created a small diversion by bringing the second scotch.

"So whatever you've been imagining," Lindsay continued when the waiter had gone again, "it's not true. Daddy's been fine. It wasn't easy for him to confess he'd lied to me all those years ago."

"I called him three months ago to talk about the possibility of having you with me for your birthday and Christmas. It took him a very long time to give me an answer."

Lindsay shrugged. "I told you it wasn't easy for him."

"I couldn't understand what was going on. My lawyer couldn't get any answer. And every time I called, I got your housekeeper and she wouldn't tell me anything. It was as if you'd disappeared off the face of the earth."

"Daddy wanted some time with me before I go to college next year."

"What about me? Can you give me some time, Lindsay?"

"I don't mean to be cruel, but where have you been for the last fourteen years? If you wanted time with me, you sure let a lot of it get by without any contact at all."

"It seemed..." Phyllis' throat closed up and she paused to regain her composure. "It always seemed that there was plenty of time. You see, I always pictured you as three years old. I hadn't kept pace with your growing up. I wasn't expecting a young lady."

"How very odd."

"I'd like to see you sometimes," Phyllis said wistfully. "If I come, will you see me?"

"Yes, of course, I'll see you. I'd like to get to know you better. It'll take a while to get acquainted, I guess. But I know you're a good person. Daddy wouldn't have married you otherwise."

"I'd like to see him again."

"I don't think there's going to be time this trip. We're leaving tonight."

"So soon? I had hoped we could do some things together. Maybe you could spend a few days with me if Keith has to get back. You could fly home a little later."

"I'm sorry. I'm the one who has to get home."

Phyllis tried not to sound as forlorn as she felt. "I see."

"I'd better go upstairs now and finish packing." Lindsay stood up and smiled as at a stranger. "Goodbye, Mother."

Phyllis looked up at her, forcing herself to smile. "Goodbye, Lindsay."

Lindsay walked quickly away. Upstairs, Keith stood at the window, looking out at the cheerful holiday lights, seeing nothing but Lindsay walking away from him. He turned when he heard the door open and was astonished when she flew to him and threw her arms around him, tears coursing down her cheeks. He held her close, the fear of losing her only slightly abated.

"Here, now," he asked softly, "what are you crying about?"

"Can we go home, Daddy? Right now? Tonight?"

"Didn't it go very well, Sweetheart?"

Lindsay dashed into the bathroom for tissues. After mopping up, she went back into the sitting room and flopped down in an easy chair.

"I don't know," she said, replying to his question. "It went okay, I guess. I don't want to talk about it now. I want to go home. To see

Alma and Pepper and Scott and Sue and Pat and everyone."

The weight Keith had been carrying lifted from his heart. "Sure we can go home. Right now."

They drove all that night until finally, shortly before dawn, exhaustion forced them to stop in Boise. Lindsay slept until nearly eleven and let her dad sleep until noon. Then she banged on the communicating door and had her suitcase in the trunk before he joined her for breakfast in the coffee shop. Keith was delighted that she was anxious to get back home -- back to the home he had made for her.

They didn't talk about Phyllis until they were past Tubb Springs, going down the last long gradient into the valley. The moon was bright, reflecting the snow on the mountainsides. Keith was driving and Lindsay was so quiet that he thought she was asleep until she turned to him and asked a question.

"What was Mother like when she was young?"

"She was sweet and very beautiful. What's she like now?"

"Her looks are pretty well gone -- she drinks a little. She's nice but kind of bitter."

"That's too bad."

"Daddy, may I ask you something personal?"

"If it's too personal, I can not answer. Go ahead."

"Why haven't you ever married again?"

Whatever he'd expected, it wasn't that. He thought a moment before he answered. "I don't know. Fear, I guess. The burnt child fears the fire."

"Do you like Sylvia Markham? I mean, I know you like her. What I'm asking is, why don't you ask her to marry you?"

"You know, Sweetheart, I've kind of been thinking along those lines myself. I've missed her so much, I must be in love. Do you think she'd have me?"

"She'd be crazy not to."

"There are those who would say she'd be crazy if she did."

"Home," Lindsay said, looking across the hills. "Orgasmic. It seems like we've been gone for years." She cast a glance at her father. "When I go to college, you're going to be alone, you know."

"That fact hasn't escaped me," he smiled.

"Dad, let's go out to the house you and Mother started to build."

Keith was surprised. "Now? Why?"

"Please? I want to."

"Why not?"

A few minutes later he turned onto the road

that led up to the site he'd chosen so carefully for the home that would house his dreams, his and Phyllis'. He parked and looked around at the stacks of lumber and the pile of fireplace stone. The moonlight shown down on the skeleton of the house, making it look new and hopeful instead of weathered and dreary. He and Lindsay got out of the car and stretched. Lindsay ran and jumped up on the subfloor, warped now by rain. Keith climbed up beside her.

"I never told you about this house. How do you know about it? Sue Pohl again?"

Lindsay laughed. "Not this time. Everyone knows about this house. They say it was your masterpiece and you couldn't finish it because of your broken heart."

"Wow. That's almost as romantic as a curse with spectral hands and rattling chains."

"Yeah. It could be your masterpiece."

"It's a good house. Do you think Sylvia would like it?"

"I think you ought to ask her."

The next afternoon, after a good long sleep and one of Alma's home-cooked breakfasts that seemed like heaven after weeks of restaurant meals, Lindsay was in the back yard playing with Pepper when Keith came out the back door. He was going to the office for a couple of hours to start getting acclimatized to regular work again. Scott came out the Markhams' back door to help his mother who was reaching into the back seat of her car to pick up a bag of groceries. Keith got there first and without looking around Sylvia handed him the bag and reached for another. Keith straightened up with the groceries just as Scott punched him, catching him on the cheekbone. Being slightly off-balance, Keith went down, cans and fresh vegetables rolling all over the driveway. He sat on the pavement looking at Scott in blank amazement. Sylvia backed away from the car to look with distress from Keith to Scott and back again.

Scott stood over Keith with his fists balled. Keith looked at Sylvia as if hoping she would explain her son's behavior and saw that she was wearing a much-needed maternity smock. He scrambled to his feet and took her by the arms, his face reflecting his delight. Sylvia was bewildered. Lindsay and Pepper joined them just as Allison and Geoffrey opened an upstairs window and began to holler encouragement to Scott. Pepper began to bark joyously at all the excitement after such a long spell of calm. Alma came out the back door and stood with her hands covering her open mouth, aghast at the show of raw emotion.

"Is that my baby?" Keith asked, searching Sylvia's eyes for clues to her feelings.

"Now see here," Scott interposed. "You can't treat my mother like that. Get her preg -- just leave for months at a time and expect to come back and take up where you left off."

Scott grabbed Keith by the shoulder but Keith shrugged him off.

"Not now, son." He turned back to Sylvia. "It is, isn't it?"

She nodded and he folded her in his arms.

"Will you marry me?" Keith asked, softly.

Scott tried again to separate them. "You let my mother alone. This family's had about enough of you."

"Later, Scott. What do you say, Sylvia? I do love you so, please say you will."

"I don't know," she said dazedly, the whole situation having taken her by surprise and having previously made up her mind that she was about to become an unwed mother at the age of thirty-eight.

"Say yes!" Lindsay cried.

The twins joined in, "Say, yes!"

Sylvia looked around at them all. She smiled and put her arms around Keith's neck.

"Yes."

About the Author

Barbara J. Olexer was born in Klamath Falls and is a fourth-generation Oregonian. Her formative years were spent in small towns --Tulelake, California, Ashland, Oregon, and a logging camp called Wetmore (Camp 5) in Wheeler County, Oregon. She went to high school in Fossil and Tulelake. Barbara's life has been a tapestry of changes as she has lived and worked in small Oregon towns and some of the country's biggest cities, such as San Francisco, Hollywood, Baltimore, and Washington, D.C. She has written more than twenty novels, nonfiction books, and screenplays. She has been a dental assistant, housewife, farmer (near Malin, Oregon), receptionist, secretary, writer, and publisher. After many years working for a nonprofit organization in Washington, D.C., she has joyfully returned to the Northwest, where her children and grandchildren live. She and her husband reside in Milwaukie, Oregon, with their two cats.